SMEK
FOR PRESIDENT!

-GRUNT

Also by Adam Rex

The True Meaning of Smekday

SMEK FOR PRESIDENT!

By Adam Rex

Art by Adam Rex
with Keeli McCarthy

DISNEP • HYPERION

LOS ANGELES   NEW YORK

First Edition, February 2015
10 9 8 7 6 5 4 3 2 1
G475-5664-5-14319
Printed in the United States of America

Library of Congress Cataloging-in-Publication Data

Rex, Adam, author, illustrator.
  Smek for president! / Adam Rex.—First edition.
      pages cm
  Summary: "Gratuity Tucci and her alien friend, J.Lo, journey to New
Boovworld, one of Saturn's moons, to clear J.Lo's name after a string of
misunderstandings"—Provided by publisher.
  ISBN 978-1-4847-0951-1 (hardback)—ISBN 1-4847-0951-9
[1. Human-alien encounters—Fiction. 2. Extraterrestrial beings—Fiction.
3. Interplanetary voyages—Fiction. 4. Adventure and adventurers—Fiction.
5. Science fiction. 6. Humorous stories.] I. Title.
  PZ7.R32865Sme 2014
  [Fic]—dc23   2014010764

Reinforced binding

Visit www.DisneyBooks.com

For Henry

ONE

I heard our back door open, and J.Lo plunged through in a snit.

"The peoples in this town, they sure do hold a grudge," he announced. "You accidentally make ONE PUPPY colossal and suddensly you are *'that alien.'*"

I have to admit I didn't stir from the sofa, or even look up from my magazine. I'd heard all this before. "You just have to give them more time to get used to you."

"Used to me? Used to *me*? I am already used to *them*, and there are manies more of them to be used to."

"Everything will calm down once they catch the puppy."

"But in the meantimes I grow them a perfectly good new community center out of cornstarch and not even a thank-you!"

I laid the magazine in my lap. "Your cornstarch community center melted," I reminded him. "In the rain. All those Cub Scouts—"

"Yes, yes," J.Lo replied with an impatient wave. "Well . . ." he added, deflating slightly. Literally deflating—it's a Boov thing. "It serves the Club Scouts right for not letting aliens join."

"So what happened today?"

"Oh . . ." J.Lo shrugged, or tried to. He doesn't really have the shoulders for it. "It was just this man on the corner. I should have jaywalked that street. The humans laws cannot tell a *Boov* whats to do."

"I bet the police would disagree with you. And you've spent enough time in court lately."

J.Lo plunked down on the footstool. "I am a rebel," he whispered. "Prisoner of a world that does not understand me."

"You're somethin', all right."

"A *prisoner* . . ."

I'll admit I'd been feeling a little like a prisoner myself lately. About a year ago we'd moved out of the city to a quiet part of the Poconos. General Motors had paid us a lot of money for a good look at our flying car, Slushious, and we'd spent most of it on a nice house near a lake. It was so nice and quiet and peaceful and calm that I sometimes wanted to scream and break things. I'd grown up in a city; I was a city girl. It was weeks before I could get used to sleeping without the sounds of people honking at one another.

So I said, "If you really feel that way, we should go somewhere. Mom may have to work, but I have nothing to do until September."

J.Lo fell off the footstool. But he came up strong. "Yes!" he cheered, pumping his arms. "New road trip!"

"They're still rebuilding Happy Mouse Kingdom," I said, rousting myself. "But we could go to the beach. Or Arizona! We completely trashed the place during the occupation, so it would be nice to spend some of our Slush Fund there."

"Is 'Slush Fund' a name you just now made up to call our Slushious-car dollars?"

"Yes."

"Sweet."

"We totally missed the Grand Canyon back when we were in Arizona," I added. "We could see that. Or New York City—I'm gonna live there one day anyway, so I may as well check it ou—"

"NEW BOOVWORLD!" said J.Lo. "New Boovworld! Final answer no takebacks!"

"Oh," I said, sitting again. "Yeah? New Boovworld."

"We will see the HighBoovperial Palace, and then to the Museum of Noises, and I hear through my nanowave radio that they have rebuilt the Mysterious Bridge."

"What's so mysterious about it?"

"It is actually a hat shop. Also it has a twist ending!"

"Yeah?" I said. "What's the twist?"

J.Lo frowned, and made a little twirl with his finger. "It . . . curves at the end. Am I not using that word right?"

"J.Lo," I said, in a tone of voice I hated as soon as I heard it. "J.Lo, is all this really a good idea? You on New Boovworld?"

His face fell. And turned mauve, slightly.

* * *

I saved the world a while back. J.Lo and I did, that is—we forced these big aliens called the Gorg to leave Earth before they'd destroyed it with their huge purple ship.

Now, before you say anything: I realize you've probably read Dan Landry's book, *Just a Hero*, and you know that he took credit for the whole thing. He got super famous for it, as you can imagine. Well, I let him. One day I intend to be a super-famous author myself, and if I want to be sure people really love me for my books, I have to let Dan Landry have this one. Every time I publish something, I don't need people saying, "It's a good read, a real page-turner, but you know what thing of hers I really liked? That time she saved the world."

So I'm really only writing this for practice, and so my biographers will have stuff for their research after I'm dead. People always tell you, "Writers write," and after you get over the urge to say "No duh," you realize they just mean you gotta do it every day, even if you don't have any good ideas. Whatever. Practice.

You know who didn't get enough writing practice? Dan Landry. Not to be mean, but I don't think real autobiographies are supposed to have so many exclamation points.

So maybe you haven't read his book. Maybe everyone eventually realized that he used too many adverbs, or that he stole his whole climax from *The Last Starfighter*. Maybe you read some *other* book that got the Smekday Invasion wrong, or saw that animated movie they made about it. Whatever your deal is, you probably think you know all there is to know. And if that's what you think, you don't.

So let me get you caught up.

I guess I *must* have gotten famous if you're reading this, right? The late, great Gratuity "Tip" Tucci. Or maybe you're just a sneak.

Anyway:

Everyone in America got moved to Florida.

Welcome to FLORIDA

Except the people from Florida—they got moved to Ontario for some reason. I didn't find that out until later.

I decided I could move my own self; so I loaded my cat, Pig, into the car and drove us out of town.

And I had a smallish-to medium-sized accident.

And met J.Lo in a convenience store.

J.Lo souped up my car, and we drove to Florida, but the humans weren't there. Turns out the Boov decided they liked Florida after all, so they sent everyone to Arizona.

And I learned that J.Lo was actually hiding from his own people because he'd accidentally sent this crank call to their greatest enemies, the Gorg,

so now the Gorg knew about Earth.

And then the Boov found us, and there was a car chase until the Gorg ship appeared in the distance and scared the Boov away.

Then we were sad for a bit.

Then I decided nuts to that and we started out for Arizona to find my mom and kick the *Gorg* off my planet.

And we had a smallish-to-medium-sized accident.

And while the Boov and *Gorg* fought, we got our hands on a *Gorg* telecloning booth—which is something the Boov had never managed to do. No one understood how the *Gorg* had figured out how to clone and teleport themselves.

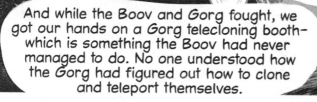

Then the *Gorg* took some time off from shooting every cat on Earth to go looking for their booth, which was in a junkyard owned by this guy everyone called Chief Shouting Bear.

I met one of them face-to-face, which is not the way to do it,

and he sneezed when he got close. Even though J.Lo said the Gorg never get sick.

And the Chief had a smallish-to-medium-sized accident.

But he was okay, and J.Lo and I used a crashed Boovish ship to fix the car, and drove the teleclone booth to Arizona so the Gorg wouldn't find it.

And in the end Dan Landry claimed to have made the Gorg leave Earth by defeating their champion in this cage-match dealie that was conveniently free of witnesses, so whatever.

"Don't get me wrong," I told J.Lo. "I think the Boov should *love* to have you visit. I think—"

The doorbell rang. Our Great Dane, Lincoln, came galloping out of the laundry room, barking and trailing a meringue of dog slobber. "Hold on," I said, and got up. "Lincoln? Lincoln? Lincoln! Sit! Siiiiit. Good boy."

There was a college girl out on the porch. I didn't know for sure she was a college girl until she turned to leave and I saw that her short-shorts said DUKE across the butt. I hope that's what that meant.

"Is this where the *Boov* lives?" she snarled at me before I could even say hi.

"I . . . think he lives in this neighborhood," I told her. "Why?"

"He *tackled* me outside the yogurt shop! Look what he did to my boots!"

She showed me her furry boots by way of pointing one leg straight at me, like a rifle. They looked kind of mangy, as if someone had been ripping clumps of hair out. And they were perforated in a way that was pretty consistent with J.Lo's dental pattern, so.

"Try the blue house on the corner," I told her. "Good luck!" And she turned and stormed off without another word. Lincoln trotted back to the laundry room.

"All right, what was *that* about?" I asked when I returned to the living room. J.Lo was petting Pig. "Why did you attack some girl's boots?"

J.Lo looked incredulous. "She is still mad about this?" he huffed. "I *told* her—I *thought* they were *ankle*wolves."

"Okay, whatever. I—"

"Why elsenow would a person wear fur with shortpants? It makes no sense!"

"I'm past that now. My point from before is: I think the other Boov *should* want you there. They should give you a parade. But all they know is that you're the Boov who signaled the Gorg. They'll lock you up, or make you shovel koobish poop or whatever."

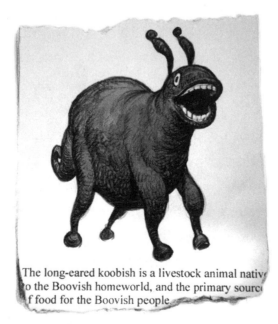

The long-eared koobish is a livestock animal native to the Boovish homeworld, and the primary source of food for the Boovish people.

J.Lo twiddled his fingers. "Sometimes I think I should make up a time machine," he said. "Like in your moviefilms. Go back and un*do* that stupid Gorg signal."

I just nodded and didn't tell him what I thought of that. That I really believed that everything had happened in practically the best possible way. Without the Gorg, the Boov would have just kept pushing us around. I don't know if we *ever* would have gotten rid of them. But then the Gorg came and spooked the Boov, and we found the Gorg's Achilles' nose, and in the end the humans got their planet back. The Boov never really understood how we got the best of the Gorg, but they agreed to make a new start on one of Saturn's moons. Everybody won. Why mess with that?

"They do not poop, the koobish," J.Lo said. "By the ways."

"Okay."

"They release wastes as a spray of tiny particles, aslike air freshener."

"I didn't ask."

J.Lo winced. "But not . . . *exactly* like air freshener, if you catch what I am saying—"

"You can't really build a time machine, can you?"

"Eh. Probablies not. The amount of power required would be ridicumulous. But! Next best thing is go unto see Captain Smek! Explain about the cat clones! If he understands, maybies he will let kiss and make bygones."

"But you'll never get within a mile of the palace. They know your face."

"I cans wear my old helmet up with the glass darkened! No one will know."

"That won't look a little conspicuous?"

"Nah, lots of peoples does it. Is like sunglasses."

"I don't know."

J.Lo gave me a look. You've probably never seen this look—I don't know if the human face can even do it—but it is as sad as a baby in a rainstorm.

"I am some kind of crazy celebrity," he said. "Hated by alls the Boov for to what I did, hated by alls the humans for what the Boov did do."

"What? No human hates you," I said. Though I didn't believe it. "After the Latin Grammys last November* you were actually kind of popular. For a while." That much was true—he'd even been a guest on some talk shows. And I'd watched those talk shows, and made nervous fists whenever I'd thought the audience was laughing at him instead of with him. I can make my hands hurt even now, just thinking about it.

"You did not hear this man today," said J.Lo. "At the crossedwalk. He told to me: 'you are *that alien*.' Like *that* he said this."

There. I was making fists again. "Well," I muttered. "I hope he got hit by a truck."

"No you do not do."

"Too harsh?"

"Too harsh."

"A truck carrying pillows then," I said. "A pillow truck."

"I wonder now," said J.Lo, "if there has ever before been such a person as me. The fink of two planets."

I thought, One planet and a moon, but it didn't seem like the time to nitpick.

The doorbell rang again. Lincoln scrabbled out of the laundry room, barking and oozing things from his face, and pawed at the door until I got him to sit.

"Good afternoon, miss," said the shorter of the two police officers on the porch.

"Hi."

"We've had a complaint against the Boov known as J.Lo?"

"Uh-huh."

"For shoe biting?"

"Right."

"Do you know his current whereabouts?"

I sighed. "He went to New Boovworld," I told them.

TWO

If you ever want to schedule some quiet time to think about
what a bad daughter you are, may I suggest the silent inky
blackness of space? If you're like me, you'll really get to
feeling like garbage right around the boring stretch between
Mars and Jupiter.

And yes—as a matter of fact, I *do* mean boring. When we
shot up through the atmosphere, I think I was about as excited
as I've ever been my entire life, and looking out the back
windshield at Earth, round and blue and perfect looking? Super
nice. But after that it's just black. You can see a lot of stars, but
they're all so far away that you can't even tell you're moving.
So sue me—eventually I just drifted into the backseat, buckled
myself in so I wouldn't float around, and read.

"We should have teleported," I said.

"Hm. Very tricky, teleporting so far," J.Lo answered. "A person would need a burly transmitter."

"I don't think 'burly' is the word you want. Powerful?"

"Yes. Very powerful. Or else the signal gets degraded acrost such a distance."

He got a weird look on his face, like this line of thought troubled him. I didn't ask why. *I* was the one who'd just left a note for her mom that read *Gone to Saturn—call you when I get there,* so I figured I had enough troubling me.

Like our last conversation, for instance.

* * *

"What?" she'd said. It was really the only thing she'd been saying for ten minutes, which I was beginning to understand was a bad sign. It was totally ruining dinner.

"Just a little trip," I told her. "A day trip."

J.Lo whispered, "It will take a day just to get to there—"

"Just a little three-day trip," I explained.

"What?" It didn't even sound like a word anymore. She was a bird of prey, all big-eyed and screechy.

"You let us take a trip together over spring break," I reminded her.

"Okay, this is *nothing* like going to Philly," Mom said, getting polysyllabic all of a sudden. "This is very . . . very different. Very. How would you even get there?"

"Slushious," I told her.

"The *car?* In space. No."

18

"It will require some souping," J.Lo admitted.

"I didn't even have to tell you," I said. "I could have said we were just going to Philly again."

Mom dropped her fork. "Oh, you are *not* helping your case."

"All right," I agreed. "That was a dumb thing to say."

Mom went back to eating—cramming it in, really. Chewing madly with a frown on her face. Mom has never believed in spanking, but she doesn't mind showing you what she can do to a ham sandwich if it really gets on her nerves.

"But come *on*," I told her. "You're really going to be like this? I was on my own for *six months* after you got abducted the first time. I drove *three thousand miles*."

"You got shot at, too. So I guess I should let you join the army?"

I groaned. "No one wants to join the army—"

"I'm just trying to figure out the new rules, Tip. Apparently anything you did during the invasion is something you're allowed all the time now, is that it? I mean, if I hadn't wanted you to drive a car then, I should have thought of that before getting abducted by *freaking aliens*, pardon my language."

"Freaking aliens," repeated J.Lo.

"Oh!" Mom added, sweeping her arm in his direction. "And J.Lo tells me you ate nothing but vending machine food for a week. So I guess that's okay too, 'cause apparently I don't get to be your mother anymore."

"What?" I coughed. "No one said that."

She looked down at her plate. "You've been saying it all year. In little ways, you've been saying it." She pushed her baked beans around with her fork. "J.Lo, I'm sorry I called you a freaking alien."

"Is okay. I am sorry for saying you have poodle hair."

Mom twitched. "When did you say that?"

"Beforenow, when I saw a poodle. You were not there."

Usually when J.Lo said something like this, Mom and I would share a glance. A *you just heard that too, right?* kind of look. Instead, she lifted her head and gave me a hard stare.

"Look," she said. "I know I wasn't Mom of the Year before the Boov came, but I am *all in* now."

I shrank back into my chair. "I know."

"End of discussion," said Mom. "J.Lo, please pass the salt."

"This is the chlorine. The salts is in front of you." He put a little chlorine on his deodorant sandwich.

Mom shuddered. "We have to start labeling things."

* * *

I didn't even really *want* to go to New Boovworld. I thought it would be too much like a party where I didn't know anybody. But now that I suddenly wasn't allowed to, it seemed kind of important. So over the next few days, while J.Lo rebuilt Slushious, I built up my case. If only to myself.

"I just feel like I've earned this," I told J.Lo while he tinkered. "Earned her trust, I mean. I'm thirteen years old. If I'd lived a thousand years ago, I'd be married and have kids and be dead already."

"You are singing to the preacher," said J.Lo.

"Preaching to the choir," I corrected him.

"Yes. This thing."

He was futzing with these crazy-big thrusters he'd attached to the back of the car. *He* didn't need Mom's permission. Now that his mind was set on hashing things out with Smek, he was going with or without me.

"You know I practically took care of *her* before the invasion, right?" I added. "She had me when she was pretty young. I think in her mind she was still the community-college girl whose life I ruined."

"Tipmom does not believe you ruined her life," said J.Lo as he cranked on a bolt. I stood behind him, feeling kind of hovery and unhelpful. The garage door was open, and the garage air thick with dusty light. J.Lo had piles of tools and garbage everywhere. At least three unfinished projects stood or leaned or lay indecently on the floor with their hatches open. Mom knew to park her Honda in the driveway if she didn't want to find it suddenly glow-in-the-dark or fitted for skis.

"Whatever. Anyway. At some point during the invasion Mom turned into a, I don't know, responsible person. Like a reverse werewolf. I can't get used to it. She's got all this newfound *Mom*ness, and she likes to try it out on me every time I want to do anything fun. Well," I said. "If I'm all grown up earlier than she wanted, it's her fault, is what I'm saying."

"Tip should do now whatever Tip is wanting to."

"Uh, pretty much, yeah. Right."

"If Tip to wants to take a trip, Tip should trip."

"Basically."

"If in schooltime Tip wants some schooltime off, she takes it off."

"I know when I need a personal day."

"If she says, 'I am going to spend my college fund monies on a baseball ball—'"

"It was signed by *Jackie Robinson*!" I said. After a moment I added, "It was supposed to have been signed by Jackie Robinson. Okay, that one might have been a mistake."

J.Lo finished draining the car's oil and started spraying some kind of foam up in there.

"We got most of my money back," I reminded him.

He didn't say anything.

"I mean, 'Jorkie Rombison' . . . what kind of name is that?"

"Tipmom warned you about the baseball ball," J.Lo mentioned with a kind of verbal shrug.

"Yeah, well," I said. "She's an expert, she's been scammed so many times." I paced. "She couldn't even see through Dan Landry's act, you know? So."

In the silence that followed, it was hard not to notice what an amazing spaceship Slushious wasn't. Still too much Ford Falcon and not enough *Millennium Falcon*.

"So isn't the car a little leaky for space travel?"

"Ahanow. Watch," J.Lo said. He clapped, and a glassy film shot out from the base of the thrusters to form a bubble that enveloped the entire car. Or almost the entire car—there were little round gaps here and there. J.Lo frowned, clapped again to retract the bubble, then clapped a few more times until he finally had a solid casing.

"That inspires confidence," I said.

"It only needs adjusting. It will be ready."

"And what if we feel like applauding something on the way?"

"We will have to try not feeling like that," he replied. "Wait. 'We'?"

"Yeah," I said, chewing my lip. "Mom'll let me go; you'll see."

* * *

"Looksee," said J.Lo now, in space. I sat up and found him pointing out the passenger-side window. "Jupiter."

I guess we weren't passing very close. It looked like a distant moon.

"Do you want me to take a picture?" asked J.Lo. "For Tipmom? Not every humansparent has a picture of her daughter posing with Jupiter."

"That's . . . okay," I said. "She knows what Jupiter looks like."

I felt like J.Lo was eyeing me. He said, "I guess she does do."

"It's just that she doesn't think space is such a big deal," I added.

"This is why she changed her minds about you going, probablies."

"Probably. I didn't ask."

"Yes. But you *did* ask her again if you could go. Of course."

"Of course."

"I am only checking."

"Sure."

I hid behind my book again. J.Lo coughed.

"Because when we *left*," he added, "she said, 'Have fun at Splash World.'"

"That was a figure of speech."

"Ahyes. I am still so bad at those."

* * *

New Boovworld used to be called Titan, back when it was just one of Saturn's moons. And let me make up for all my wet blanketyness earlier by telling you that Saturn is *breathtaking*. It's totally ridiculous. You might as well be flying toward the whole idea of space.

Does that make sense? Ask a person to draw "space" and they're gonna draw a planet with rings around it. Going to space for the first time and getting to see Saturn is like visiting America and watching a bald eagle plant a flag on top of the Statue of Liberty.

After we'd learned that the Boov were going to leave Earth for Titan, the Chief had taken J.Lo and me to look at Saturn through a telescope they had on the university campus in Tucson. It had looked hazy, pale—it wasn't the best telescope, and there are much better pictures of Saturn in books. Still, there's something about seeing it with your own eyes.

"My turn," J.Lo had said, fidgeting.

"My people called it Séetin," said the Chief. "Until the white man stole it from us and renamed it."

I turned away from the eyepiece and frowned at the Chief. "Until . . . what? How can that be true?"

The Chief was smirking. "It isn't. I'm just messing with you."

And now, as we skimmed over the planet's icy rings, I said to J.Lo, "I wish the Chief could have seen this."

He'd died over a year ago, at the age of ninety-four—just a few months after the Boov had left Earth.

"I do also," said J.Lo. "He would have liked Saturn."

I wiped my eyes. "Or, you know, he might have yelled at it to stop blocking his view of Uranus," I said. "You could never tell with him."

"Yes."

I spotted New Boovworld then, just a dot in the distance. There was something off about it.

"Is it . . . It's inside a bubble too," I said.

It was opaque enough that you could just barely see the moon concealed inside, like a toy from a bubble-gum machine. They'd enclosed an entire world. For protection?

"It's for helping warm up," said J.Lo. "Is cold, this far from the sun."

I suppose it was—we'd been running the heater the whole way.

We couldn't just fly into the bubble, apparently. We'd have to park Slushious on the outside and leave her there while we took a bus down to the surface.

"Remembers," said J.Lo. "We are in parking spot number -π/73034."

He pulled the car forward until its bubble touched the bubble that surrounded New Boovworld. Then they kind of stuck together, and merged. There was a round opening where they intersected.

"I don't like this," I said. "I thought we'd have the car down there."

"It will be fine. EveryBoov uses public transport when he can."

"It's just that we have kind of a history of leaving places in a hurry. Happy Mouse Kingdom that one time? And Roswell? We even had to hightail it out of Philly after you said the Eagles were lazy."

"I only meant *actual* eagles. Those mens misunderstood."

Through the hole in the bubble I looked out through the clouds to the yellow surface of New Boovworld. It was making me feel sick, this perspective. I was looking directly out the windshield but I was also . . . looking down? Like straight down at the planet? We were far higher than any airplane, twenty miles up. There weren't any other spacecraft parked immediately to either side of us, but I could see some other little Boovish cruisers anchored in the distance. J.Lo always liked parking Slushious by itself so it wouldn't get any door dings.

J.Lo gazed down at New Boovworld too. "Looks like

they have really fixed the place up nice," he said.

He was wiggling a lot, looking kind of fluttery. I guess he must have been excited. I didn't see him signal or anything, but almost immediately this long hot dog of a ship approached, curving along the inside of the sphere.

"Whoop," said J.Lo, and he followed this with the Boovish word for helmet. The familiar fishbowl snapped up all around his head. Then he said something else and it turned blue. You had to really be looking just to make out his gray face through the tint.

The hot dog ship pulled up and halted with a sound like *chshhhhh*. I guess buses make that noise no matter where you are. Through the long tubular bubble of it I could see a few other Boov holding on to straps above their heads: Boov in rumpled outfits, with tanned faces, back from vacation. Another Boov in a shiny rubber uniform stepped from the front of the bus onto a little platform.

"Maap ba pop umana," she said.

"Ba-aaaaaa," J.Lo answered. "Map."

"Habana?"

"Pa-pop Smek Wanyeah."

"Wah maaaaa maa pop aaah ba muhambanay," said the Boov. "Pop pop. Ha ha manaah ah gom humaba ma-ah naaaaaaaaaaaaaaaaaaaa pop ruh snap pop gah-ha baaa pop blan pop mam wan hamba hamba hamba muhna mam am mnaaaaaaaaaaaaaaaaaaaapopaaaaaaaaaa sumaminay."

"Map," said J.Lo.

She stood aside and motioned us onto the platform.

We stepped inside the bus and held on to a waist-high bar as it got moving again. The Boov in the uniform came alongside me with something like a hot-glue gun in her hand.

"Muhaha ba snoo pop pop baaa," she said, and I flinched when she brought the little gun up to my spine.

"OW!" I said as a sharp pain took root in my neck.

"Ham tamaa sahpop ha but if pain persists or he develops garblemouth he should see a doctor."

"She," said J.Lo. "Tip is a girl."

"Really," the Boov replied, looking me up and down. "Weird."

I reached up to touch the spot where I'd been burned, and my fingers found a new little mole there, right on my backbone. We were descending through the clouds now, and with nothing else to look at, the Boov on the bus were all staring at me.

The Boov who'd mole-gunned me looked at J.Lo and asked, "How much benzene can she drink?"

"No amount of benzene."

"She will have then to take these pills. And this is her collar."

She handed J.Lo a white plastic collar with a round metal dog tag, and he handed it to me. I just stared at it.

"What," I said.

The Boov eyed me. "Is the translator not working? *This. Is. Your. Collar.*"

"Tip, please to put it on. You are *embarrassing me*," hissed J.Lo.

"Fine," I sighed, and fastened it around my neck. "Guk," I added as the collar tightened itself around my throat.

I tried being angry about it, but the truth was I'd noticed something that made me want to cut J.Lo a little slack: when he'd spoken to me, he'd switched to English. Even though the mole made it so he didn't have to. It was just one of those pointlessly polite little gestures, like holding someone's car door or blessing sneezers. It was sweet.

"Please hold on to the handrails provided," said the driver, in Boovish. "We will be on the surface shortly."

Meanwhile, I had no idea what my dog tag said. The translator mole didn't seem to work on the written word. J.Lo had made me a bunch of Boovish flash cards that I'd been meaning to get around to studying, but I was still pretty much illiterate.

The shuttle rumbled, slightly. Then we made a real gut-pumping drop below cloud level, and I got my first good look at New Boovworld.

The nicotine-yellow surface was blistered with buildings that looked like they were made of glass and rubber. Bony plastic towers pointed like fingers at the sky, next to fat plastic globes and marshmallow shapes. A few of the structures looked like grounded ships—like they used to be the same kind of big hose ships that once filled the skies over Earth but were now moored and spreading their tentacle roots into the Titan soil. Next to these, little orb houses clumped like caviar. Geodesic cloning towers overlooked a kidney-shaped patch of green, dotted with fleshy trees and covered in dark little shapes. Dark little moving shapes.

I pointed. "Are those koobish?" I asked J.Lo.

"Yes. Happily grazing. I cans not wait to eat myself a piece of one."

"You will have to wait," said a Boov behind me. "There are no koobish on this shuttle bus." He waved his arm at the rest of the shuttle bus to prove his point and yep, no koobish. "You will have to wait until we land, and then you may locate a suitable koobish, and eat part of that koobish."

"I know this," said J.Lo. "I cannot wait."

"But you will *have* to wait," said the Boov.

I ignored them and watched the window as we neared the surface. The air above was fizzy with bubbleships. And still more bubbles were arranged like constellations overhead: bubbles stacked to form slender columns, bubbles grouped like a solar system, a huge bubble trailing dotted lines of bubbles like a jellyfish. I knew from the Boovish occupation of Earth that these were probably just signs. Huge billboards spelling words and phrases in the spaces between the towers—towers that stretched so sharp and tall, like they were aching to pop something. And the Boov were building downward, too: an open chasm revealed brawny struts, thick pillars, and subbasements, and sub-subbasements, and sub-sub-subbasements. All of it a gaping mouth, spewing weird gases. And everywhere, lakes. Dark steaming lakes with tattered edges, connected by crooked little rivers.

"But you will *have* to wait," the nearby Boov was saying, and J.Lo broke away to join me at the window.

"New Smek City," he said. "The national capital."

"Man," I said. "You guys name *everything* after him."

J.Lo shrugged. "He has been HighBoov all my whole life. He will be HighBoov until he dies."

We landed in an open square. Well, not a square so much as a nonagon. Filled with Boov, and signs, and advertisements and, around the edges, lines forming in front of open holes in the ground.

It was all very, very orange. The sky was lit like a dying jack-o'-lantern. The sun hung just over the horizon, directly between two icicle towers, as if it had been installed there. And on the opposite side of the sky: Saturn. Just hanging out, no big deal. Its rings tilted crosswise like it was propped up on its elbow. Practically winking at you.

Then my view of Saturn went wobbly as a trail of Boovish bubble letters settled in front of me—sort of a transient billboard or something. So I looked around some more, at the people.

I saw my first Boov kid. A teenager, maybe—looking lost, reading signs, blinking a lot. It was a little shorter than the others, with just the slightest nub of tadpole tail sticking out the back of its head. I saw Boov in rubber uniforms, Boov in T-shirts I couldn't read, a Boov leading this little flying armadilloey-looking thing on a leash. I seemed to be in everybody's way. They bumped into me, but Boov are mostly air—I outweigh your average Boov by like sixty pounds—so it was kind of like walking into the middle of a pillow fight.

Or maybe I should say that I outweigh a Boov by sixty pounds on *Earth*. The gravity was totally different here. I took a step and ended up doing the long jump into a cart selling M'Plaah milk.

"Tourists," muttered someone.

"Sorry," I said, picking up the milk bottles. "Sorry."

It was hard to tell with his helmet all dark, but J.Lo seemed to be watching a sign like a huge TV. I walked gingerly over to him and tested out my vertical leap.

"Ohmygosh," I said. "I think I can dunk. I think I can dunk and there isn't a basketball court for a billion miles." Then I took a huge misstep and ran into a drinking fountain.

J.Lo helped me up. "How is this not bothering you?" I asked.

"Eh, the Boov, we are used to these changes. We repressurize our air bladders, we retain a little water; it sorts itself out." He looked back up at the billboard.

"Is that Smek?" I asked. I recognized the fancy clothes.

"Yes."

The ad played a loop of the captain smiling and waving, smiling and waving. There were shapes all over it, too, but of course I couldn't read those.

"What does it say?"

"'Four more years,'" said J.Lo. "That is strange."

"Just four? Is he retiring?"

"Wellnow. Remember that New Boovworld is in orbit to Saturn. Saturn's year is aslike thirty Earth years."

"Wow, seriously? You mean it takes New Boovworld thirty years to go around the sun."

"Yes."

"So . . . what's so strange about Smek wanting four more years? That's gotta be the whole rest of his natural life."

J.Lo was still watching the screen. "Not strange that he wants this. Strange that he is asking."

Then the Smek ad went wobbly and that same string of bubbly letters got in my way again. Like it was following me around.

"It is following you around," said J.Lo.

"What?"

"Some billboards? If they are noticing you looking at to the same place for more than a couple of moments, they are designed for to block your view."

I tried to turn my head, and the bubbles followed. "So

why does it seem like it's only bothering me?" I asked.

"Every other Boov knows to waggle his head and blink a lot. Confuses the signs."

"*You're* not doing that," I pointed out.

J.Lo reached up to tap at his helmet's dark glass.

"Oh," I said. "Right."

There were other ads—some kind of skin cream, a carbonated drink that apparently makes your head bigger, even an ad starring Dan Landry. It was hard to follow without the captions, but the message seemed to be that he'd defeated the Gorg thanks mostly to a particular brand of breath spray.

"This way," J.Lo said, taking my hand. He led us to a line of Boov who were waiting in front of one of the holes in the ground. J.Lo pointed to the sign over the hole. "HighBoovperial Palace," he said.

I squinted at the alien letters, trying to remember what it meant if a big bubble had all those little bubbles queued up along the edge of it, when suddenly that same billboard got in my way again.

The line was moving, steadily. We'd take a step forward every few seconds toward whatever was going on up front—I hadn't been paying attention. Now I watched as a light winked on over the hole and the Boov at the front of the line dropped into it.

"Whoa," I said, stepping back. "What?"

FOOMP, went the hole. The light snapped off for a second, then back on again. The next Boov stepped over the edge.

FOOMP.

"I know that sound," I murmured. It was the sound a big bubbleship made when it sucked a person up one of its hoselegs.

The Boov ahead of us in line turned and smiled. "Is it his first time on New Boovworld?"

"Yes," said J.Lo from behind his helmet. "She has never traveled by sucktunnel beforenow."

"So cute at this age. Still teething?"

This would have made me madder if I hadn't had a permanent tooth coming in on the right. I touched it with my tongue.

"Still teething," said J.Lo. "Makes her fussy."

"It does not," I muttered.

The Boov ahead of us was next. "Byenow," she said, and fell into the hole at her feet.

FOOMP.

"We have to go separate," said J.Lo, stepping forward. And I didn't even have a chance to respond before the light lit and *FOOMP,* he was gone.

"Uh," I said.

It was just a dark, whooshing hole. The thin accordion sides of it flapped from the suction.

The light came back on.

I stepped. But then I didn't step.

"It is your turn, human," said someone.

I turned and gave an apologetic wave to all the Boov behind me. I was a Barbie doll all of a sudden—stiff smile, couldn't seem to bend at the knees and elbows.

"Humansboy! Step inside the sucktunnel."

"Sorry!" I said. "Sorry. Just gimme a second. I've never done this before."

"The tallest neckbird may choke on a single stone, human!"

"What? What does that mean?" I muttered. "Is that a fortune cookie or something?"

"Many fingers make a hand," said someone else.

"Okay," I said. "Okay. On three."

"The longest journey begins with a single person pushing you," said the next Boov in line, before pushing me.

FOOMP.

And I went, "EEEEEEEEEEEEEEEEEEEEE!" I've thought of cleverer replies since then, but that's what I said at the time.

I whipped feetfirst through the sucktunnel, banking through curves, turning slowly along my axis like a pig on a spit. It was utterly dark, so I can't really tell you what it looked like, or even how long it took—I think I kind of left my body for a second. But a year or possibly three seconds later I *foomp*ed out the other end of the tunnel and then *SMAP,* I was stuck to a safetypillow—one on a spinning pink wheel of safetypillows, which swung me around and popped me loose on the side opposite the tunnel. I landed on my feet, barely, and pinwheeled my arms around for balance. "KEEP MOVING," said an electronic voice, so I hopped forward just as the wheel turned and the pillows dropped a Boov where I'd been standing a moment before. I glared at him.

"You didn't have to push me," I growled.

He walked by as another Boov dropped from the safetypillows behind him. "I have never seen you before in my life," he said.

"Oh." I checked out the next Boov as the pillows swung another one around. "Did you push me?"

"It is possible; I have pushed many humans," said this new Boov. "When would this have been?"

"Aha! Never mind, it was that guy!" I said as another Boov arrived. "I recognize his little . . . zipper thingy. You pushed me!"

"No," he said, "I make a point *never* to touch humans—that's how you get hooties."

"Man," I sighed. "You Boov all look alike."

"That's racist," said the Boov, clucking his tongue. He left, and I was alone.

Finally I stumbled through a door into a sort of Grand Central Station, where J.Lo was waiting.

"What kept you?" he asked. "Tunnel clog?"

THREE

This room was vast and tall, vaulted with hoops of blue glass that made the orange light outside look halfway normal.

"I love it here," I told J.Lo. "I'm already making friends."

"Seenow? I told you."

"So is this it?" I asked him. "The HighBoovperial Palace?"

"Do not be ridicumulous. This is a sucktunnel terminal. The palace—"

Suddenly there was some Boov guy in our face. "YOU THERE, FRIEND WHO WALKS WITH A HUMAN! Do you not agree that New Boovworld needs a modern leader for a modern age?" he shouted.

"The palace is probablies . . . this way," J.Lo finished, sidestepping the shouter. "What is this business?"

"A capable leader, a DYNAMIC-STYLE leader! One who is not content to rest on his laurels!"

J.Lo gasped. So did a lot of nearby Boov.

"What's the problem?" I asked.

J.Lo lowered his voice. "We do not talk about a person's . . . *laurels*. They are *private*."

I gave my new mole a poke. "I'm not sure this thing's working right."

The Boov doing all the shouting was standing atop a little platform that he appeared to have brought and inflated himself. Above his head were some letters, spelling something, and a floating image of a Boov in a green jumpsuit with a flag undulating in slow motion behind him.

"PONCH SANDHANDLER is the leader we need! Respected by all for her-his excellent sandhandling, she-he could have been the fanciest officer in the Boovish fleet."

Everyone made thoughtful noises.

"And yet now! SURPRISE! Ponch Sandhandler volunteered for the *Four Hundred Thirty-Seventh Floating Infantry!*"

This was super impressive, apparently—everyone recognized that division. "The Furious Fightpunchers," someone whispered.

"This is very strange," J.Lo told me. "It is almost aslike he's saying this Sandhandler ladyfellow should be HighBoov. Instead to Smek."

"Eh," I shrugged. "Somebody's always yellin' somethin'."
Then my view of the speaker was blocked by a cluster of
bubbles.

"GAH!" I shouted, waving them away. "Another one?"

"The same one, actualies," said J.Lo. "It seems to have
followed you here."

"Say 'NO MORE' to the HighBoov who needed a humans
man to fight his Gorg for him! The humans have a saying:
'See ya—would not want to be ya.' The HighBoov should be
as an inspiration, but who would want to be Smek now? Elect
Ponch Sandhandler!"

His voice faded from our ears as we exited the terminal
and walked, blinking, into the sunshine. I squeezed J.Lo's
shoulder pad for balance. Only by sort of mincing along could
I keep from launching into terrible gymnastics.

"It's following me, isn't it," I said.

J.Lo glanced back at the billboard. "Yes."

It was like a dog. Like I let it finish my sandwich and now
I was going to have to ask Mom if I could keep it when we
got home.

I sighed. *Mom.*

There was a patch of mossy green here that smelled like
swimming pool. A dozen koobish grazed amid plush-looking
palm trees. J.Lo plucked the tip off a koobish's ear as he passed
and chewed it pensively. I'm probably never going to get used to
seeing that, but the koobish couldn't have cared less.

"Some bonkers things happening here, I can tell you," J.Lo said.

"What, because of that speaker back there?"

"Because therenow is an uncertainness. An uncertainness about our leadership. This is not the homeland I was remembering."

"It's a whole new *world*," I told him with a wave of my arm and consequently a fall to the ground. "Ow."

"A whole new world," repeated J.Lo.

"Yeah. I know people say that and they just mean they bought a new phone or found a diet soda they really like, but this is literally a whole new world. It makes sense that things would change. Plus the Gorg are leaving the Boov alone for the first time in, what—a hundred years?"

"I never thought I would have seen it."

"You're not just seeing it; you helped make it happen," I said, smiling. "And soon Captain Smek is going to thank you personally."

The palace was right ahead of us. It was one of those buildings that had been built out of an old starship. Through the pumpkin-colored haze I saw a big bubble dome up top, then a couple of stories like a gleaming coaster underneath, then hoselegs snaking wide, rooted to the ground or forming breezeways between buildings.

I hadn't seen much of Boovish art, apart from the stuff J.Lo draws. I guess when you're always in exploration-and-battle mode you don't have a lot of time for nice things. But here I could see what the Boov had done to this former spaceship now that they had some time on their hands, and it looked like it had been decorated by a bunch of ten-year-old Japanese girls: lots of round, cutesy animal shapes, bright colors, mirrored trinkets, and plastic fins sticking out every which way. And here my memory abruptly ends because the palace got hidden behind a billboard. Whatever.

"Change is good," I said, maybe a little blithely.

"Ha," J.Lo huffed.

"What?"

"I have been watching the Americans. You like to think you decide things, but you only ever decide not to change. Because you are afrightened of change. You are the man who likes a big menu but always orders hamgurbers."

I frowned. "Come on. You're freaking out just because your people are *thinking* about changing leaders. We have a presidential election every four years."

"Ah, and what a *crazy amusement ride* this is," said J.Lo, wiggling his fingers. "Remembers when you elected that really fat lady? Or that Hindu man? How 'bout the unmarried short guy?"

"Or the *black man*?" I answered. "How about that time we elected the black man."

"Eh, a fluke. Your presidents cans not even have a beard anymore. He cans not even have a *hat*."

I tried to think of how to answer this, and while I was thinking, we entered the palace through an open hoseleg that was only half buried in the foundation. The ribs of it formed arches over our heads as we walked through the hall. Thin light filtered in through the accordion membrane and gave everything a kind of milky sameness.

I looked up and all around, so of course I caught a glimpse of that bubble billboard floating behind me. I thought I saw how it worked, kind of. In the center of the billboard was a plump little silver doodad—a floating chrome Christmas ornament with six spindly legs and a pair of wiry antennae and a fat trumpet in the back where the bubbles came out. The Boov called them bluzzers. During the invasion we humans called them bees. Some were microscopic; others were pickle-sized like this one. There were bees for tracking people, bees for exploding and sabotaging things. And bees for advertising, apparently.

I looked it in its three little eyes. If those even *were* eyes. And as I watched, it changed its message—just for an instant, but it changed. Like it was a secret between it and me. I found myself wishing that I knew what it was trying to tell me.

But that was ridiculous—it was a *billboard*. A *commercial*. As a little kid I'd always had a habit of giving personalities to every little thing. I'd talk to the faces in the electrical outlets.

I'd try not to have favorite outfits because I didn't want any of my clothes to feel left out. I would have starved if only you'd made me name all my food before I ate it.

I jerked my head at the billboard and asked J.Lo, "What is that thing even trying to sell me, anyway?"

"Eh," said J.Lo as he tried to think of how to explain it. "Is a kind of strap for people whose eyes are too big. Aslike a bra for your face."

"Super."

At the other end of the hoseleg hallway was a checkpoint—probably a metal detector or whatever the Boovish version of a metal detector would be. A pleasant-looking Boov wearing what appeared to be shingles was flanked on either side by serious guards. It was only then that it hit me what a stupid idea this was. It was like we were walking up to the White House gates and asking for a sit-down with the president. I think it hit J.Lo, too.

"Hello, visitors!" said the pleasant-looking Boov. "Welcome to the HighBoovperial Palace. Your billboard will have to stay outside."

"Don't tell me," I said. "Tell it."

The pleasant-looking Boov opted not to do that. "Are you here for the exhibit on how a bill becomes a law?"

The Boov motioned toward the exhibit—which was in Boovish, English, and Chinese—but it was just a picture of Smek thinking hard with a caption that read:

1. A BILL IS PROPOSED.

2. CAPTAIN SMEK DECIDES IF IT IS A LAW OR NOT.

"Huh," I said. "Is that it?"

"Of course that is not it. On the opposite side there is a microphone for asking for new laws! And a button that says 'no' when you press it. Would you like to 'take it for a spin,' as I'm told you humans say? You are forbidden to actually spin it."

司馬軻队长 • Captain Smek

"No, please," said J.Lo. "We would like to . . . see Captain Smek?"

It was quiet for a bit after that. The guards looked at each other.

"We, um, do not have an appointment."

I smiled a wan little smile. "Pretty cray-cray, huh?"

"Yes," said the Boov, looking at an agenda. "Normally this would be considered big-time cray-cray. *Normally* we would have some funny neckties we'd make you wear for suggesting such a thing. But . . . you are here at the luckiest time."

"Yes?" J.Lo looked hopefully at me. "Are we?"

"Captain Smek is trying to be"—the Boov tilted its head—"more available to the little persons this week. A dynamic, listening sort of HighBoov."

"Uh-huh," I smirked. "Wonder what could be bringing *that* on." J.Lo elbowed me.

"Yes. So." The Boov affixed a sticker to J.Lo's helmet and another to my dog tag. "The pink lift will take you to our great leader. Kabaap."

They moved aside, and J.Lo and I stepped through. I shot a final glance over my shoulder at the bubble billboard. It was hanging back a bit. And I thought it looked nervous, because I'm an idiot like that. I gave it a frown and a curt wave.

This section of the palace was like a vast hollow ring,

with gently curving corners that were buttressed against the ceiling. Light came in a hundred portholes and through the rafters. More Boov dressed in shingles walked this way and that, as tubaharp music faintly played.

"My mole didn't translate the last word that Boov said," I told J.Lo. "It sounded like . . . 'kabaap'?"

"Ah. It is like . . . 'good luck, you are going to need it.'"

"Oh. And the stickers we're wearing?"

"They only to say 'visitor.'"

We got on the pink lift and it shot us up so fast my legs almost gave out. We rose up and out of the elevator shaft and kept going through the open air of the great glass globe that formed most of the palace—past platforms bustling with Boov, past smaller globes and big pearly baubles that must have been private offices. All of it gleamed, apart from a spaghetti of dull orange tubes that connected everything to the coaster section below. We shot up and up to nearly the highest point of the globe. Then the door of the lift opened, and we exited onto a dizzying skywalk.

It was transparent, which was bad enough, but then it didn't have any side rails either. I looked down and immediately wished I hadn't. Below was a kaleidoscope of crystal curves and moving bodies. As we stepped, our footfalls sent ripples through the skywalk, as if the whole thing might disappear if I stopped believing in it.

So I was super happy to pass through a door and into a

saucer-shaped room with a solid floor and walls. There was a solid desk here too, and a receptionist who was as solid as any Boov. Which is to say not exceptionally solid.

"Greetings, brother!" said the receptionist as she stood. "Plus one. The checkpoint monitor said you would be coming. Is this your first time calling on our Beloved Leader?"

"First-time caller, longtime listener," said J.Lo, in Boovish. Not that you could see his face, but he actually seemed kind of excited. Bouncy. "Is he in there? Can *we* go in there?"

The Boov smiled. "You will have to lower your helmet."

Blue-headed J.Lo said, "But I do not want to lower my helmet."

The receptionist's smile zippered up a notch. "But you will have to. You will have to do that."

"But I do not want to."

Clearly this had never happened before.

"This has never happened before," said the receptionist. "In my . . . in my position as secretary to Captain Smek it is my responsibility to ask visitors to remove their helmets. Or hats. I have other responsibilities. Sometimes I am sent for pastries."

"I understand," said J.Lo.

"It was in my capacity as secretary to Captain Smek that I asked you to remove your helmet. Before. Sooo . . ." she said, twirling her hand at the wrist.

One of the nodes atop her desk winked on.

"Ms. Yogurt!" said the voice of Captain Smek. "What is all that mumbling out there?"

"There's a mysterious Boov to see you, Captain."

"Interesting! Sounds mysterious! Why is he mysterious?"

"I can't see his face, sir. He won't remove his helmet."

"Ms. Yogurt, it is one of your responsibilities as secretary to *ask* him to—"

"I know! I know, sir! I did ask him, but he says he does not *want* to remove his helmet."

"Fascinating. Can you put him on?"

The receptionist covered the node with her hand. "He wants to speak with you," she told J.Lo.

"Hellonow," said J.Lo.

"Am I talking to the mysterious Boov who doesn't want to remove his helmet?"

"Yessir."

"Would you please remove your helmet?"

"No."

"Well, I'm flummoxed," said Smek. "This has never happened before."

"I told him that too, sir."

"Maybe," I offered, just to keep things moving, "maybe you could let us in anyway."

"Was that you, Ms. Yogurt?"

"No, Captain. The Boov has a humansboy with him."

"Girl."

"A humansgirl!" said Smek. "Well, I've got to hear this. Make them wait the usual amount of time and then see them in."

"Thank you, Captain," said the receptionist. She motioned for us to sit in a little waiting area. "Captain Smek is in an important meeting right now, but he will be with you shortly."

I was prepared to say something, but J.Lo took my wrist and led me away. So we sat.

Everything was very white. People tell you purple is the color of royalty, but don't let them fool you. If you really want everyone to know how rich and powerful you are, you make everything clean and white. Only respect and money can keep it that way.

All the magazines were in Boovish, apart from a *Ladies' Home Journal*. My chair wasn't really designed for humans, and it was stickier than I like.

After about fifteen minutes, the receptionist pattered over.

"The captain will see you now."

FOUR

We'd been in the office of the HighBoov for maybe a minute and a half, just J.Lo and me, and I still hadn't spotted Captain Smek. It was a really big room. Imagine you're an ant in an ostrich egg. Or maybe that's not helpful; just imagine you're in a really big room.

The Boov called it the Oval Office. J.Lo insisted that the office of the HighBoov had *always* been called the Oval Office and that it was just a coincidence. It was maybe seventy feet wide and at least a hundred feet tall, and the walls were made of all these rippling layers of frosted glass that were kind of disorienting. A thick pillar rose up from one end of the room and tapered off to a nub just below a skylight, high above. At the base of the pillar was something called the Great Seal of the United Boov, which was also a coincidence, and which in this case was an actual seal. They'd brought it back with them from Earth. It was pretty great, though. In the corner was also a parrot and an aquarium full of lizards.

I leaned closer to J.Lo, to the tinted blue helmet that concealed his head. "So how long do we just stand here—"

"*Shhh!*" J.Lo scolded. I was getting impatient. So far nobody but the seal had said anything.

Then the top of the tall pillar opened up like some weird flower, and there was Captain Smek. He was holding a long, hooked baton and sitting atop a blue, pillowy chair. Let's call it a throne. When you design an entire room around a single chair, I think it's safe to call it a throne.

He adjusted his hat, which looked like it would honk if you squeezed it, and pressed something on his armrest.

Suddenly a huge hologram filled the space between us.

"Aah!" I said. J.Lo fell over and bonked his helmet.

A blue, shimmering Smek head as big as a doughnut shop addressed us:

"MYSTERIOUS BOOV AND HUMANSGIRL. HELLO."

"Hello!" said the parrot.

"HOW CAN THE VERY MODERN AND CAPABLE LEADERSHIP OF CAPTAIN SMEK MAKE YOUR LIFE BETTER?"

You could squint up at the top of the pillar and see that this hologram was just a projection of whatever Smek's actual head was doing. J.Lo said, "Helmet," and the blue glass fishbowl around his face snapped back down beneath his collar.

"Oh great Smek! The mysterious Boov is me! I." He leaned in toward me. "Me or I?" he whispered.

"You can tell if you rearrange the sentence," I told him. "Would you say, 'Me am the mysterious Boov?' Or would you say, '*I* am the mysterious Boov—'"

"But that is not how we do it in Boovish."

"Then why did you ask me?"

J.Lo turned to face Smek. "The mysterious Boov am I!"

"I CAN'T UNDERSTAND ANYTHING YOU PEOPLE ARE SAYING," said Smek. A thin pole rose up out of the floor between us. "SPEAK INTO THAT."

"I am the mysterious Boov," said J.Lo, pointing to his face. "Me."

"SHOULD I RECOGNIZE YOU?" Smek leaned forward slightly in his chair, and so the hologram head lunged forward several feet until it was rubbing noses with J.Lo. Metaphorically—neither Boov had much in the way of a nose. "I MEET A LOT OF PEOPLE, YOU UNDERSTAND. AND YOU'RE *VERY* FAR AWAY."

"Far away, bwak!" said the parrot. "Bring me a Danish!"

"Maybe you should just come down here, then!" I shouted.

"COME DOWN . . . COME DOWN THERE. HMM."

"Just a thought."

"NO, NO—IT'S"—(sigh)—"IT'S EXACTLY THE SORT OF
FRESH HUMAN THINKING THAT ENABLED DAN LANDRY
TO DEFEAT THE GORG, I'LL BET."

"This is kind of what we were wanting to talk to you
about," said J.Lo. "Actually."

"HOLD ON."

The hologram winked off, and the flower thing closed up
over the throne again. I shifted around on my feet, waiting.
The parrot filled the silence by asking for kisses. A few
moments later there was a *ding*, and the captain appeared
from around the back of the pillar.

He gave the Great Seal a pat as he passed, and ambled
across the gleaming white floor to meet us. Then he gasped.

"You!" he said, pointing at J.Lo.

"Yes."

"Younow!"

"Me."

"The Squealer!"

"The *Squealer*! Bwak!"

J.Lo cringed. "If . . . this is what people are calling me . . ."

Captain Smek poked his hat. "Security!"

"Wait!" I said. "No. Just hear us out."

"But I've already poked the hat."

"We just want to tell you what really happened to the
Gorg," said J.Lo.

"We didn't have to walk in here like this," I said. "We could have just sent an e-mail." I winced at J.Lo. "Why didn't we send an e-mail?"

"Ten minutes," J.Lo pleaded.

Captain Smek sighed and poked his hat again. "Never mind, security." He looked squarely at J.Lo. "You have your ten minutes."

Which wasn't a lot of time, as it turned out. We did our best. J.Lo would falter; then I'd pick up the thread; then he'd fill in the parts I couldn't explain; then I'd tell the parts he wasn't there for. And let me tell you: our story does *not* work as a ten-minute anecdote. It sounds like a joke told by a four-year-old that you just know he's making up as he goes.

Still, Smek was rapt throughout the whole thing. You could tell he was really thinking—he even started asking questions. By the end he was leaning up against the seal, which had fallen asleep, and tapping his teeth with the fat tip of his frog finger.

Then we finished, and no one said anything for a while. Smek was staring over our heads, tapping, tapping.

"It, uh, sounds ridiculous, we know," I said.

"No," said Smek. He looked at me. "It makes more sense than that Dan Landry's story. We never could figure *that* out."

"Landry's a poomp!" said the parrot.

"So you believe me?" J.Lo said, bouncing just a bit on his little legs. His head was fluffing slightly, like it did when he was really happy.

"You are still the Squealer," said the captain. "You still brought to Earth the Gorg."

"Yes. I know." His head collapsed a little, like a soufflé. "That business . . . that was some crazy fluke, I tell you. The signal should *never* have been so burly. I . . . I cannot explain it—"

"But if the Gorg *hadn't* come," I said, "then I—then *we* wouldn't have learned their weakness and sent them packing. They'll probably never come back! This whole solar system's got 'bad neighborhood' written all over it now."

"A remarkable story," said Smek, thinking. He looked just like his portrait in the exhibit downstairs. Like at any moment he might veto something. "Makes more sense than Dan Landry's story, but is still hard to believe. The people would not swallow such a story without a leader to tell them to."

J.Lo and I looked at each other. I couldn't tell how well we were doing until Smek poked his hat again.

"Security!" he commanded in a clear voice.

"Wait," I said. "What?"

"Security!" said the parrot. "Security!"

"Why security?" asked J.Lo, stepping back. "Whynow?"

"To detain you," said Smek, coolly. "To take you to the detention nub in Sector Three. They can lead you out down the beige elevator, I think—past all the cameras."

"You don't believe us?"

"No, I do," said Captain Smek. "I *do*. And you've backed

me into quite the pickle corner, as you humans say."

"We don't say that."

"You've heard of all this election nonsense? *Some* people think they should get to decide if I stay HighBoov or not. *Some* people think this Sandhandler should be leader."

"Sandhandler's a poomp! Bawk."

J.Lo looked like a leaky pool toy. He was all squinched up and blinking. "But I . . . I am loyal to *you*, captain," he said.

"And I thank you for your vote."

I narrowed my eyes. "But . . . J.Lo's worth more to you as Public Enemy Number One," I said. "There's nothing in it for you if you tell the truth."

"Public Enemy Number One," said Smek. "That is good. Do you mind if I use that?"

"If you put J.Lo in jail, then you get to be the leader who caught the Squealer."

"I am so happy you understand."

The only sunny side here was that the security guards still hadn't shown up. I glanced behind us, to the door where we'd come in. Captain Smek noticed too, and poked his hat a few more times.

"Guh," he groaned. "We switched to a new hat provider, and the coverage is just . . . I couldn't be more disappointed."

"Time to go, J.Lo," I said, and grabbed his arm. Good thing, too, because it was like he was paralyzed with disappointment.

Smek was still holding that long baton, and now he swung it down and narrowly missed us as I pulled us away. "No!" he commanded. "You will go only where and when and in what manner I say!"

I yanked J.Lo's arm and rushed back the way we'd come, forgot about the gravity again, and grazed my head against the top of the doorjamb as we passed underneath.

"Dang it," I said through my teeth.

"Cans not believes it," J.Lo muttered, in English. "The glorious Captain Smek."

The receptionist waved to us as we bounded through like the whole palace was an inflatable party castle.

"Was your conference with our great leader everything for which you hoped?" she asked.

"Can't talk!" I told her. "Escaping!"

"Tallyho, then!" she called. "Isn't that what you humans—"

"No one says that!"

We blew out of the waiting room and back onto that awful skywalk, and that's when we saw security finally responding to Smek's call. A little phalanx of Boov in olive-green suits and helmets rattled toward us, blocking the opposite end of the bridge. Each carried a trumpety-looking weapon in his black-gloved hands.

"Crap," I said. "Pardon my language."

"The Squealer!" said one of the guards, and the others gasped. Then they grinned, like they were already imagining all the talk shows they were gonna be on.

I looked all around, but it was pretty hopeless unless I planned to jump us both off the skywalk and onto another platform fifty feet away and fifty feet below us. I could see distant Boov on that platform, pausing in their work to watch the ruckus on the skywalk above.

"Do not hurt the humansgirl please!" shouted J.Lo. "She has not done anything!"

The guard in front raised his gun, so the rest followed suit. "Lie down now," he ordered, "and no one will hurt anybody."

I remembered those Boovish guns that just erase things. No noise, no explosion, just *boop*, your head's gone.

"If you erase us, Captain Smek will never have proof the Squealer was ever here," I said.

"Except for all the cameras everywhere recording this," said Smek, who had apparently just appeared in the doorway behind us. "But the humansgirl is right. No erasures."

The guard in front looked down at his gun. "Then . . . what setting do you want us to use?" he asked.

"What is that, the K-pop-eighteen model?"

"No sir, the twenty-two is standard issue now."

"Oh, weird, I don't know the twenty-two," said Smek. "What settings does it have?"

"Erase, Comasleep, Tummy Trouble, and Blue."

"Interesting. What is 'Blue'?"

"Turns things blue. It's pretty self-explanatory."

Meanwhile, J.Lo was trembling beside me. So I picked him up and hugged him, which was super easy 'cause in this gravity he weighed like six pounds.

"Human," barked the guard as they advanced. "Put down the Squealer."

"It's just a hug!" I said. "Not at all suspicious!"

But they might have realized I'd been lying after I took a step and leaped off the edge of the skywalk.

FIVE

"AAH!" shouted Smek. "Tummy Trouble! Fire!"

"Fire! Fire!" squawked the parrot, distantly.

Tummy Trouble sounded like nails on a chalkboard, but the guards must have missed. We sailed though the sparkling air and I felt like a superhero. Why had I been bothered by this low-gravity thing? I was amazing. I made the jump easily and landed with a roll on the lower platform.

"EEEEEEEEE!" screamed the scattering Boov, who ran for either a narrow bridge or a glass slide that connected this platform to others.

"Oh man, I really wanna try that slide," I muttered.

"Ooh!" said J.Lo. "Oooooh! My tummy!"

I set him down. "Are you okay? I thought they missed us."

"It . . . must not work on humans. Feel like I could marf."

Smek's shrill voice followed us down. "After them! The Squealer is *Public Enemy Number One!*"

"Like I could marf right out my poomp," J.Lo insisted.

I looked up to see each of the guards pull a rip cord and inflate his uniform. They swelled up all over like they were covered in swimmies and vaulted off the upper skywalk toward us. I lifted J.Lo up again and made for the slide as the guards released air valves on their backsides and shot like farting balloons across the gap. I jumped butt-first onto the slide and spiraled down to a larger platform below us. I'm ashamed to say that it was just as much fun as I thought it would be.

"I am ready to give up," said J.Lo.

Boov scattered off this platform too, mostly to an elevator off at the far side.

"Oh, c'mon," I said. "I think we're doing pretty well."

"Only a smatter of times before someone is hurt," he answered.

One Boov on this platform rushed us—looking to be a hero, I guess—so I turned him over carefully and balanced him on his head.

"WAAAAAA," he yelled, waving and wiggling his legs.

"And what if we get into the outside?" added J.Lo as he clutched his midsection. "Where could two such as us hide?"

He had a point there. And even though he was being nice about it, the real problem was me and only me. They wouldn't

even have to put a description of me on the wanted poster—
they could just say "human."

"I will go into jail," said J.Lo. "You will be sent home. And
at home you can send e-mails to New Boovworld, asking for
my release. E-mails to this Ponch Sanderson, maybies."

"You should listen to him," said the Boov on his head.

This *was* beginning to make sense, and I don't know
what I would have decided if I hadn't looked up just then
to see the security guards. They were on the disk above,
gathered around the edge, and pointing their weapons
straight down at us. I didn't want to find out what another
blast of Tummy Trouble might do to J.Lo, so I grabbed him
and hurtled us toward the center of our platform just as the
Boov fired.

Over the screech of the weapons I could hear one of the
guards shouting. The barrage ended and he was still telling
the others, "Not all at once! Not all at once! Too much sonic
will—"

He was interrupted by a deafening crack.

A sliver of our platform's glass disk was suddenly shot
through with silvery webs—and then it shattered, musically,
and the glittering shards of it dropped from sight. And the
crack spread.

"Oh, jeez," I said as I grabbed J.Lo's arm. I took off
running and the crack ran behind, and I dove off the opposite
edge of the platform.

"Oooooooooooooh," J.Lo groaned.

We tumbled downward, in slow motion, as another firecracker echoed above. I caught a glimpse of a bridge coming up fast, managed to get a toehold on it to push against, and launched us off in a new direction. And now we plummeted onto a globe suspended below, hitting the upper curve of it with a smack.

The chunks and splinters of the ruined platform above us showered down, smashed the bridge I'd just touched, and barely missed the big glass globe we were clinging to. We listened to the debris break a few other things on the way down and finally crash onto the roof of the coaster section with a sound like every waiter dropping every dish in every restaurant in America.

I'd lost my wind for a second. "Ow," I said when it came back to me, my face smooshed against the glass. And then *SQUEEEEEEEEEEEEEEEEEEEEEEEEEEEEEEEEEEEEEEEEEEEEEEE EEEEEEEEEEEEEEK*, we slid, and I dragged an oily faceprint down the side of the globe. With my free hand I managed to slow us down a bit.

"You okay?" I asked.

"I am okay. I marfed a little and it made me feel better."

Boov inside the globe were staring up at us. One of them did something complicated with his fingers.

"That is a very rude gesture," said J.Lo.

Captain Smek and his inflatable commandos floated

down to meet us now, seated on little scooters. They looked just like the antler scooter J.Lo had when I'd met him, and they made *putt-putt* noises as they hovered there. Smek had his baton. He bomped me a little on the head with it.

"Quite the chase," he said, bomping. "Quite. The. Chase! But who could expect less from Public Enemy Number One?"

"Yes, sir," said a guard.

"Would you leave us a moment, officers?" Smek said to the other Boov. "I would like to have with the Squealer a private word."

"Sir?" said the same guard. "Sir, he is dangerous—"

"Just move a little ways away, that's right. Just out of earshot. I won't need long."

I couldn't see them very well without turning (and probably falling), but several of the *putt-putt* noises faded until one stood out distinctly from the rest. Smek hovered closer and holstered his baton. He folded his arms on the scooter's handlebars and leaned his chin against them, like he was just hanging out with the young folk, like he might at any moment ask if he could "chill" with us a while. He reminded me of the youth pastor at my church who nobody liked.

"An unfortunate situation," he told us. "No easy solution."

"I am ready for prison," said J.Lo, and my heart sank a little. "The humansgirl has a little carship parked outside to the shell. It can take her home to Earth."

"So I should just let her go is what you are saying?" asked Smek.

J.Lo struggled to turn his head. "She has . . . she has not done anything."

"Gratuity," said the captain. "It is Gratuity, yes? Forgive me, but humans all look the same. You are young?"

"Yes!" I answered, and the movement of my face made us slide a little. "Yes. I'm young. Can't be tried as an adult and . . . so forth."

"I suppose you have told all your little friends this story about world saving and Gorg and cats, yes?"

"No, actually. You see, I didn't want people to—"

"Interesting. But you will tell people now, won't you."

I suddenly felt like the Tummy gun might have done a number on me after all. "No! I would never—"

"I will bet you are so young that the humans would say you were a foolish and irresponsible humansgirl to come here with this Boov," said Smek. "I will bet they'd believe any *sort* of terrible accident may have befallen such an irresponsible girl."

My heart was pounding.

"A tragedy, yes, that a humansgirl should have such a bad, bad accident on another world. But believable. What do the humans say? That it is 'one of those things'?"

I sighed. "We do say that," I admitted.

"You will have then to kill me too! I tell you," said J.Lo.

"J.Lo, shut up!" I hissed.

"*No I will not!* Shut up. I will talk and talk!"

"No, see," Captain Smek was saying. He practically bounced in his seat, he was so eager to tell us this part. "You won't. I thought of it upstairs. What is the perfect punishment for a squealer?"

He gave us a moment to guess. "Um—"

"To make it so he can never squeal again!" Smek answered himself. "*And* to put him in jail, of course, but we will take out your talkbox! Surgically. The punishment fits the crime! And also keeps you quiet forever—is that not clever?" He turned to the guards. "Okay, men! You may return."

"J.Lo," I sighed.

"Yes."

We took each other's hand and pushed off the globe.

I turned as we fell and made a desperate grab for the ridge at the bottom of Smek's scooter. It tipped, and sank, and I lost my grip but immediately grabbed hold of the handlebar antlers of one of the Boov guards' scooters that had cruised up underneath.

One hand holding J.Lo's, the other aching as I clutched the handlebar, I smiled weakly up at the guard. He scowled down at me.

Other scooters circled around, and other guards aimed their guns.

"Do not shoot! Do not shoot!" said the guard above us. He

waggled his hands and must have shifted his weight on the scooter, because suddenly the whole thing was toppling over. The guard came tumbling down and plowed into my head. Now the entire scooter was upside-down, and the guard fumbled for a grip, and then each of us was hanging from a different section of antler handlebar as we slowly sank.

The other Boov dove to meet us, but J.Lo reached high and flicked something on the scooter's handlebars, and we shuttled away and ever downward until we skidded to a halt against another glass saucer in the dead center of the palace globe.

We all came disentangled from the scooter, which turned a couple of circles on its side and then righted itself ten feet away. J.Lo wrestled with the guard, but the guard was a *guard*, and he soon had J.Lo facedown on the floor with a gun to his head.

The other guards were closing in.

"Go!" shouted J.Lo. "*Run!* Save yourself. Then come back and save me!"

I stood there, frozen.

"RUN!"

So I ran, God help me, to the empty scooter. Pardon my language. And I knew I'd never figure out how to fly the thing, so instead I took it by the antlers and spun it around over my head. All the way around, then around again, and then I hurled it into the middle of the little constellation of Boovish guards hovering there and got what I think you call a 7-10 split. Bad if you're bowling, pretty good if you're just trying to distract the pins while you run away.

I ran to the far edge of the platform and looked down.

"I'm sorry, J.Lo," I said, and I jumped.

SIX

I'd listened to what J.Lo had said about running. Where could someone like me hide? I was the only human on New Boovworld.

That's not true, actually. I'd learn later that there was a Human Embassy here, with a staff of like eight people, plus some college types doing research or whatever. Not a single one of them looked anything like me, not that it mattered. The HighBoovperial police were never going to sound the alarm for my arrest, because in another five minutes I was going to officially die.

Anyway. I'd hurled a scooter at those guards, like I said, and raced to the edge of the platform I was on, and thought to myself that if I got shot, just got shot right now and fell to my stupid death, I'd deserve it because I was turning my back on a friend. Literally turning my back.

There was another curvy bauble down below that I thought I could probably reach. Then slide off that to the disk beneath it. Then I didn't know what.

"I'm sorry, J.Lo," I said, and jumped.

Seemed like most of the civilian Boov had run, or had been ordered to leave. But I could see more guards rising up on scooters from the coaster level as I landed on the curvy glass and slid—and then I was falling through a hole in the roof that hadn't been there before. One of the guards must have fired his eraser gun.

I dropped into a big glass room and landed like an understuffed pillow on the floor of some Boov's office. Some important Boov, I guessed, since the office had the kind of frosted walls that meant you could pick your nose in private. If you wanted. And you had a nose to pick.

So my first thought was to pull the old hide-in-the-ventilation-ducts trick and hope the Boov didn't watch the same spy movies I did. Like, in those movies there's always an air vent you can reach from a desk, and it comes right open without a screwdriver or anything, and the good guy can pull himself right up into the ceiling even if his whole deal is that he's supposed to be an ordinary man thrust into extraordinary circumstances and probably doesn't do that many chin-ups.

Anyway. I couldn't see an air vent at all. What I *did* see was a clutch of chubby houseplants and an aquarium full of balloonafish. A curvy white desk that you sat in the center of like the yolk in a fried egg. A photo of the Boov's friend, or girlfriend, or boyfriend, or boyboygirlfriend or whatever. And next to the desk, a dull orange canister.

There were sounds at the door, but I guess the door was locked? Either way, it would only be a matter of seconds before the Boov came pouring in through the hole they'd made in the ceiling. I flipped the lid of the orange canister, and inside it was just a whooshing drop. Like a sucktunnel, but smaller. And now I remembered all those orange tubes I'd noticed earlier: tubes that connected every part of the globe with the lower levels.

So I stepped up onto the lip of the canister, and dropped inside, and heard the lid clap down behind me.

And I hoped it wasn't a Boovish toilet. I didn't know what their toilets looked like.

I was sucked downward, my stomach in my throat, my body whapping against the sides of the tube. Whatever this was, it wasn't meant for transport. I barely fit, and I'm a lot skinnier than a Boov. In near-total darkness I curved this way, that way, got briefly stuck in a U-bend, then dropped into a round room full of pointy metal teeth.

Rusty rings of them were stacked big to small to form a cone: a swirling, threshing vortex of destruction that would grind anything and everything into a gross paste. Or it would have if it had been working. The whole contraption growled, its motors frustrated and shivering with rage. At the bottom of the cone was one final, chattering set of teeth—the face of a cartoon metal monster—jammed open with a big piece of rebar. Garbage was collecting in the gaps, like the monster wasn't flossing. And beyond all this, through the gaps, I could see a little bit of light.

So, with nothing better to do today, I squeezed through the jaws and fell onto a big mound of garbage.

It was really hot in the garbage pit. There was a weird humming somewhere. Probably goes without saying that I started breathing through my mouth.

Above me was a honeycomb ceiling, and the monster mouth, and a few other mouths like it, chomping away in the distance. The sides of the room were too far away to see clearly. I think I've mentioned I can't read Boovish, but most of the garbage here was food wrappers, and most of the wrappers had a word that I'd later learn means "fun size."

I lay back in the garbage to catch my breath. I closed my eyes.

It's probably going to sound like an insult when I say that all this garbage made me think of my friend Chief Shouting Bear. But if he hadn't wanted people thinking of him every time they saw a pile of hubcaps, then he shouldn't have lived in a junkyard in the first place.

Back when the Chief was alive, he and I had all kinds of long talks. Arguments, sometimes. So I don't want you to think I'm schizophrenic or anything, but I occasionally imagine the Chief and I are having one of those talks when I need a little company. And I needed a little company.

"Hey, Stupidlegs," said the Chief.

"Hey, Chief," I answered, smiling. And I opened my eyes. He was to my left, standing lightly on the surface of the trash.

I mean, he wasn't really. I know he wasn't.

I'm not crazy.

"What're you an' the Spook doing on an alien planet, kid?"

I got up on my elbows. "Technically it's a moon," I said.

"Don't play games."

"I'm hurt," I said. "Shouldn't you know everything that's going on with me? Like don't you have a big TV set in heaven where you can watch my life?"

"I do. But it also gets HBO."

I lay back down. "Well. J.Lo wanted to come here to clear his name. But we bumbled into this whole election deal and now . . . now they're going to do something so he can't talk anymore. So I don't know if I should try to save him, which seems impossible, or run home and send e-mails—"

"And the reason you didn't just send an e-mail in the first place was . . . ?"

"I know! I just said that upstairs. But I didn't think of it back on Earth and—"

"Bullhockey," said the Chief. "It's the Spook who'd never think of e-mail. His solution for everything is some crazy contraption. You thought about sending a letter. But your ma, she wouldn't have had any problem with a *letter.*"

I stared at him a moment.

"Whatever—we had a fight is all. I'll explain to her why I had to go to New Boovworld once J.Lo and I are safely home."

The Chief was inspecting some Boovish junk. Like, appraising it. Only not really. I can't emphasize enough how perfectly normal this was, me talking to him.

"Kids, they always go about everything wrong," he muttered.

When he was alive, I was always worried he'd die soon. I wasted a lot of time, worrying. Whenever I got scared about him being too old, I made these stupid jokes about him being too old.

"You forgot to say 'kids *these days,*'" I told him in an old-man voice. "You forgot to spit and say 'dagummit.'"

"Can't spit no more," said the Chief. He smirked. "Not sure when I ran out exactly, but Johnny Carson was still hosting *The Tonight Show.*"

"Well," I said. "Anyway. When I'm old, I'm going to remember what it's like being a kid."

"I remember," said the Chief. "Some days it's *all* I remember. And I'm talking about all kids, always. Throwing tantrums 'cause their ma or pa won't treat 'em like grown-ups? *That's* irony for you. Or saying 'please please *please*' like it's a magic spell. Teenagers casting off politeness like it's a chore they outgrew." The Chief coughed. Even as an imaginary ghost I couldn't think of him for five minutes without making him cough. "Only I know *you* don't fight like that," he said. "I expect you and your mom sat down and calmly looked over the charts an' graphs you'd made."

I frowned and went silent for a while, thinking. As I lay there, an empty pudding cup fell through the mouth above and hit me in the face.

I roused, and got to my shaky feet in the garbage pile. "We can talk more later, Chief," I said. "I gotta look for a way out. And get back to Slushious, and somehow pilot it all the way home to Earth, and get the president or whoever to talk Smek into releasing J.Lo before he gets his talkbox removed." Simple. I'd done harder, crazier things during the invasion, when I was *eleven*. I'd saved the world, not that anybody knew or cared. I could do this.

Something rustled down the trash hill, to my right.

Just the garbage settling, I thought.

Most of the mounds beneath most of the grinders were this gross slurry of pulpy awfulness. Only mine had recognizable cans and wrappers and paper wads and probably Boovish Kleenex or whatever they use, and I was trying to force myself to stop thinking about it when something in the trash hill moved again.

Crumpled cellophane tumbled and turned and caught the light. A metal can rolled down the slope and stopped an inch from my sneaker. I took a breath.

"So then Luke says, 'There's something alive in here!'" I whispered. "And Han says, 'That's your imagina—'"

A stalk popped up through the pile—a stalk with a single glassy eye.

"AAH!" I started, stumbling backward. I grabbed a handful of trash and threw it at the one-eyed thing—but it was all just papery scraps, and they went every which way like confetti and fell with eerie slowness in the weak gravity.

Now the eyestalk dropped below the surface again and went on the move, pushing a gopher trail of garbage in its path. Moving right toward me. I slid down the opposite side of the hill, but the thing was fast, and right in my way again. The eye resurfaced, so I kicked it until it dove.

That was plastic, I thought. Not alive after all. Then it rose up again, a little ways off, and rose up some more, dripping garbage. And now a whole little bubble pod breached the surface, and there was a Boov inside.

The eyestalk was more like a periscope, and the bubble-pod had three sets of diggers along the bottom. The bubble retracted and the Boov stepped out.

"Hello!" he said. "What sort of thing are you?"

* * *

SEVEN

I was watching TV, sitting on an uncomfortable stool inside the uncomfortable home of the Boov who'd come out of the garbage submarine. I leaned back from the screen and exhaled.

"Oh, thank God," I said. "Pardon my language."

I was rubbing my throat—because my dog collar was tight, but also in sympathy for J.Lo's vocal cords, which I didn't realize were in his armpit. I was foggy on Boovish anatomy at the time; their insides are like balloon animals and crazy straws.

"Yes!" said the garbage Boov as he came around to the back of the TV. "Is it not excellent reception? Just a tinysmall crack in the display. It is fall-on-your-face crazy what peoples throw away." He paused, and gave me a sidelong look.

"But I suppose I do not have to tell *you* that," he added.

After a little mental Ping-Pong I figured nothing good could come of telling him that I hadn't been thrown away, exactly, that I'd escaped down here on my own. "Totally crazy," I agreed. "I'm sorry, I've already forgotten your name."

"Funsize. And you are Grace!"

"Right." Grace was an old alias. When the moment came, it had been the first thing to pop out of my mouth.

Funsize wore gloves and something like a balaclava over

his head—a dark wet-suit kind of material with portholes for his eyes. He'd built a pagoda out of trash, and it was surprisingly pretty. It stood down the hill from the chomping mouths and used a rough stone wall for support. So I guessed we were underground. Beneath the palace. The tiered roofs of the pagoda were shingled with bits of shiny metal and strung all over with strips of crinkly plastic. Every now and then a gust of hot air belched through, and when it did the plastic whipped and crinkled and sounded like rain. Inside, the pagoda was damp and cool. Funsize had a water cloner and a dozen patchwork fans made out of this or that. A thick pillar ran up through the center, so he'd arranged his secondhand furniture around it. And when I say "secondhand furniture," I mean chairs without seats, a stool with a single leg that you sort of balanced on like it was a giant thumbtack, that sort of thing. When Funsize invited me in and told me to get comfortable, I chose the cushiest-looking footstool in the place, but that turned out to be just a big mushroom.

Funsize was hopping around the inside of the pagoda, showing me things, stuff he'd made from other stuff. I had no idea what any of it was supposed to be, or had been.

"So . . ." I said. "Were you thrown away too, then?"

Funsize stopped. "Yes. Thrown away like garbage. A criminal, tossed onto the scrap heap like a heap of scrap. Discarded by society."

There was a stiff little silence here, so I complimented his hat.

"Thank you. It keeps my head in."

"I really like your house, too," I said. "But I have to get out of here. I have a friend in trouble, and . . ." I sighed. "I think I'm going to try to save him."

Funsize fiddled with gadgets. "Another . . . hu-man like you?"

"No—a Boov, actually. One that I met when you guys were on my planet."

"Ahyes. And this planet . . ." he said. "It was the last planet? The one before we came to here?"

"Yeah. Earth. You didn't see it at all? Not even on your TV?"

"The television was not yet working. But . . . no offense, please, but there was no reason to look at this Earth. We Boov, we always went to a new planet, and got chased away by Gorg, and found another new planet again. Why get used to the view? No, we Boov always moved on."

"Until now, you mean."

"Yes, until now." He got kind of starey. He was careless with the gadget he was holding, and it dropped off a table onto the floor. "Now it seems we will stay." He looked at me. "I had a friend once, you know."

"Uh, yeah? What, uh, what happened to—"

"It was her job also to collect the garbage. We did this

together. We emptied the waste bins and took all the trash to the lowest part of the ship, where it would be mashed up and used for telecloning."

"Right," I said. "Wait—for what?"

I'd thought I understood how telecloning worked. You had one thing on one side, and the telecloner made more of it on the other side. But you only have to type that out once to realize you don't really understand it at all. Regardless, I'd eaten telecloned milk shakes and water for months after the invasion.

"The garbage slop is processed and made ready for teleportation to any telecloner," Funsize explained. "Then the computers rearrange it into what is needed: fuel, or food, or—"

"AAAAAgross," I said, circling the room with my hands over my ears. "Gross gross gross gross gross gross—"

Funsize covered his ears and fell into circling behind me. "Grossgrossgross! Grossgross!" he repeated, happily, until we sort of petered out at the same time.

"Ahh," he said to me. "You know, that is the sort of thing we could be doing every day if you stay down here."

"I'm sorry," I said. "I can't. I have to help my friend. What happened to yours?"

Funsize looked out a window of his pagoda. "Her punishment ended, and she was permitted to have a better job. So. I went on collecting the trash alone, until one day they built the garbage tubes, and then the trash collected itself. Still Funsize was needed to shovel the slop. But later still the Boov come here, to this new world, and now they no longer even care about reusing the slop. Now they have a whole moonful of resources to teleclone with. Now they can hollow this world out and fill it *up* with their slop. And all because of *him*."

Funsize scowled at the TV. He'd turned the sound off, but they were playing the same footage of J.Lo getting dragged off to prison again.

"This time it was *he* who told the Gorg where we were. This *Jail-oh*. *He* who led the Gorg to these hu-mans. Did you know a hu-man named Don Laundry found a way to defeat the Gorg? Now they will never come back, maybies. Without Gorg to take our planet, we will get to use our *own* planet. Now no one needs Funsize anymore."

Man, I can think of at least a couple people off the top of my head who you oughta be mad at before J.Lo is what I might have said if I hadn't minded Funsize guessing that J.Lo was that friend I'd been talking about.

"Hollow out the world?" I asked. I didn't understand this whole operation.

"Yes," said Funsize, brightening a little. Civic pride, despite everything. "The garbage is sent down garbage tubes to the chompers, where it is chomped into slop. Yes? Some of the slop is burned to power the diggers—do you hear that humming? Then the diggers dig out the world and send the dirt rubble up tubes to the surface to form hills that can be covered with fancy houses. Whatever slop is not burned fills the hollowness and prevents the planet from getting crumplepits."

"Crumplepits," I said.

"Crumplepits," he agreed.

"Oh."

He smiled—just a little fake smile, like a model for a bigger smile that hadn't been built yet. "Is very efficient, yes? The way they replace Funsize and make his life meaningless."

"Hey . . ." I said, wanting to say something. "That Dan Landry . . . he's a joke. I . . . I bet the Gorg will come back and invade you guys again real soon."

"Do you think it?"

"Sure. And you know . . . I bet the other Boov just forgot you were down here. They were probably busy with moving, and ruining all our stuff on Earth, and everything. If you help me get aboveground, and out of the palace . . . I'll be sure to put in a good word for you with Captain Smek."

Funsize gasped. "You know Captain Smek?"

"Sure."

"Are you friends?"

"Why, just an hour ago he was saying what a tragedy it would be if I had a horrible accident and died!"

"Wow! And you think he would have pity on old Funsize?"

"Why not?" I said. I got up to leave, though I didn't really know yet where I was leaving to. "You're a good guy, right? I don't know what you did to get . . . you know, sent down here in the first place, but any Boov would be impressed with all this stuff you've made. Right?"

"Right!" Funsize answered.

"And this house you've built? *Uh*mazing."

"Thank you!"

"I like it 'cause it looks like these houses they have on Earth, in Asia. Pagodas."

"Pa-GOH-das!" said Funsize.

"That's right."

"And these pagodas on Earthinasia . . ." he said.

"Uh-huh—"

"They are also secretly death rays for shooting up fiery vengeance at those smug surface Boov who have forgotten you?"

Garbage rustled in the distance. I coughed.

"You *know*," I said, "I'm going to have to look that up."

"Fine, fine. Okaythen, follow me—I will show you how to get upstairs."

EIGHT

"Fall . . . *upward*," I repeated.

"Yes." Funsize and I were standing directly underneath those chomping jaws he'd jammed open. He had what looked like a little footstool in his hands. "You will use the hoverbutt and fall upward through the garbage pipes and take just the right forks and spoons to get to the part of the spaceship building that used to be the escape pods."

"Hoverbutt," I repeated.

"Stop repeating me. Here, take it. It is made for Boov, but should work."

I took the hoverbutt. It growled like an empty stomach. "Okay, so what do I—?"

"Put it under your butt. Yes, like . . . no, not your poomp, your butt."

"This *is* my bu—"

"Put it under your butt!"

HoVERBUTT
(drawn by Gratuity)

"Okay! Jeez." I shifted the seat a little, hopefully in the right direction. Then I sort of sat on the thing, and it growled harder and held me in place a few feet above the garbage pile. The lighter trash rippled away from my cold exhaust.

I curled up and held my knees, trying to keep balanced. "Okay, and to go up? Whoa." I was already drifting upward slowly like an old balloon.

"Here now!" said Funsize. "Take the map I have made you!"

The map looked like something I'd find on a restaurant place mat I was too old for. Funsize had even drawn a crude picture of me at the start and a rocketpod at the finish.

"When you are there, press on the yellow button!" he called as I neared the chomper. "The hoverbutt will then return to me!"

"Thank you, Funsize!" I answered as I steadied myself against the chomper's trembling jaws. "Try not to activate your death ray before I talk to some people!"

"Okay! I cannot promise anything!"

But now I was through the jaws and looked up at the ceiling above me—full of holes, each hole the mouth of a garbage tube leading to a different part of the ship. I squinted at the map and counted off the holes. There wasn't a ton of light, and in the tubes there was going to be even less, but here I noticed for the first time that my dog collar was faintly luminous, like a glow stick. It would have been nice to think that the Boov had designed it that way to be helpful, but I knew it was really so they could keep track of me in the dark. I was going to have to get this collar off as soon as possible.

I was pretty sure I knew which hole to take. Like, 70 percent sure. By now I'd realized that the hoverbutt responded to tiny little changes in posture, so I tried to lean just slightly in the right direction.

It took me a couple of tries and a smack in the forehead, but eventually I was on my way.

Then I reached a fork and didn't realize I was holding the map wrong. When I came almost immediately to the top of the tube, I peeked out through the lid. Light stung my eyes—I was looking out a garbage can in a cafeteria crowded with Boov. They sat at a single winding table, or walked around holding trays laden with weird food. I ducked down quickly, the lid clanking above me, and heard voices approach. I dove as fast as I could as the lid reopened and the tube was once again filled with light.

"Going to watch the presidential debate later?" asked a Boov as leftovers rained down on my head.

"Of course," said another that I could barely hear. "Is it not mandatory?"

"I am only making conversation."

"Your conversation is poorly made."

I sighed and dropped farther, picking pieces of koobish and who knows what else out of my hair. And I don't know how I could have possibly dropped down into the wrong tube, but when the time came, I couldn't find the same fork again. So I retraced my path, or tried to, and ended up at the top of an entirely different tube, which opened into some kind of atrium. Curved, sweeping walls looking pearly beneath a bank of sunlamps. A walkway twisting beneath a slowly turning mobile of huge, bulbous terrariums, each one packed with soil, and swollen palm trees, and furry flowers, and ferns like bouquets of spindly pink fingers.

I checked the map, and I definitely wasn't supposed to be going through an atrium. I was about to dive again when I heard a kid's voice.

I'd gotten so used to the translator that for a moment I couldn't understand why this voice sounded different. Then the speaker passed my trash can—a boy. A human boy about my age, in the middle of a conversation with a human man. His voice had sounded weird through my translator because it hadn't been translated at all.

"What do you mean you're not going to?" the boy was saying. "They brought you all the way here to say nice things about Captain Smek on TV. Why can't you just *do* that?"

"Because I have a secret plan," said Dan Landry. Then he started, and looked around. "What was that clanking?"

The boy said, "I think it came from the garbage can."

"Maybe they have rats!" said Landry. "Space rats."

"I guess."

Landry leaned over the boy. "Don't you want to hear the secret plan?"

The boy was looking past Landry at an approaching terrarium. "That's all right."

Dan Landry

Landry noticed the terrarium too, and had to hunch as it passed over his head, slow as a cloud. This room wasn't designed for anyone over five feet. Meanwhile, he eyed the boy and seemed at a loss. "Are you . . . sure you don't want to hear my secret plan?"

"I'm sure."

After a moment, Landry just said it anyway: "I'm running for president! Of New Boovworld! My plan is to announce it right in the middle of the debate tonight. What a stunt, right?"

The boy was just shaking his head. "That . . . that's *never* going to work. They won't vote for you."

"Emerson, Emerson. Have a little faith in your old man. What's Smek got that I haven't got?"

Emerson gave this some thought. "Legs," he guessed. "Like six extra legs."

"Not a literal question. But don't you see what'll happen if I join the race? Smek and Sandhandler will split the Boov vote, and I'll be there to mop up the rest."

Emerson frowned. "But it's . . . *all* Boov vote, isn't it? There won't be anyone voting who isn't a Boov."

"Just a bump in the road for an experienced statesman like me," said Landry. "Smek is in a very weak position—he says he isn't, but I overheard some Boov talking about it on Level Four while I was using the men's room. Or while I was using something that I think was a men's room, anyway."

Landry looked over his shoulder. "Actually, I don't think that was a men's room."

"But—"

"Look, the leaders here aren't used to having to run for office; Smek and Sandhandler won't know what hit 'em. You know the Boov don't even have a word for politician? I used it in conversation earlier, and this mole thing mistranslated it as 'poomp.' That's like a part of the body or something."

"Mm."

"Hello, are you listening? These are pearls of wisdom; you're lucky to be here."

Emerson jerked his head up at this. "Yeah—speaking of, why *am* I here? The Internet says Take Your Kid to Work Day was way back in April."

"Sure, but your mom has you during the school year."

Emerson folded his arms. "I think you just don't want to pay for a babysitter."

I sank back down the tube again in kind of a daze. So Landry *was* on New Boovworld, and about to make an idiot of himself again. But the Boov did think he was a hero or something—maybe he could help me and J.Lo.

I found a new fork and took a tube I was certain would take me to the rocketpods, but nope—atrium again. This time another garbage can on the opposite side. Dan Landry and Emerson had been joined by two Boov, one in white, one in green.

"Are you certain?" the Boov in white asked them. "We could send to your room a fruits basket. Or they are serving koobish in the cafeteria."

"Um, no thanks," said Emerson. "I don't eat meat."

"Koobish are not made of meat," explained the Boov. "Koobish are made of koobish."

"We cherish your hospitality!" Landry said with a grin. He tilted awkwardly to one side as a bottle of chrysanthemums passed. "But I think we'll both rest before the debate. Come on, Emerson."

The Boov watched Landry and Emerson leave. The one in white waited until they were out of sight before he spoke.

"I don't trust him. You would not believe what he just did in the Level Four vending machine."

"I keep wanting to tackle them," said the Boov in green. "You are certain neither is that humansgirl that was helping the Squealer?"

"Positive. These two are males."

"I can never tell."

"Regardless, the humansgirl is dead," the Boov in white told him. "Tried to escape down a garbage tube."

The Boov in green whistled. Or something. A whistle definitely came out of somewhere. "Poor dumb thing," he said. "Chomped into slop."

"Don't let it bother you. The humans do not feel pain like we do."

I'd had enough of *that*, so I descended again.

Look, I'm not going to bore you with the details. I may possibly have gotten lost a few more times. Ten or twenty more times. Finally I peeked up though a trash lid and it looked like I was there: a long room curved away from me, filled with shiny chrome fixtures and two dozen gleaming white lanes, like somebody had started out making a bathroom and accidentally built a bowling alley instead. At the top of each lane was a rocketpod; at the bottom of each was a big cat flap—a U-shaped door sealed with clear rubber. A giant TV hung from the ceiling over the lanes, its screen blank.

There wasn't anybody in here. I guess you sometimes need to launch out of a spaceship, but hardly anybody ever launches out of an office building. I was kind of a special case.

I crawled out of the garbage can, dragging the hoverbutt behind me, and approached the closest rocketpod—the rocketpod and the little console that was standing just to the right of it.

I think I mentioned that a while back J.Lo made me these Boovish flash cards. And maybe I hadn't been studying them as often as I'd promised, but I pressed the biggest button feeling pretty confident that I recognized the word "on" and—

SHOOOOOOOOOOOOOOOOOOOOOOOOSH, the pod

rocketed down the lane, through the cat flap, and out over the city.

I'm not going to write down the next thing I said, but the thing after that was "Pardon my language."

I stumbled quickly over to the second rocketpod and the second console and, seeing the mistake I'd made the first time, I pressed just a medium-sized button and—

SHOOOOOOOOOOOOOOOOOOOOOOOOSH, the pod rocketed down the lane, through the cat flap, and out over the city.

"Wh . . . why would they have two buttons that do the same—" I muttered before the screen overlooking the pod bay flashed on and some Boov interrupted.

"Hello?" the Boov said, from the screen. He squinted. "Is that the human Dan Landry?"

"Yep!" I said, hustling over to the third rocketpod.

"Looks like you are doing some evacuating!" said the Boov. "What a colorful human thing to do! Please stop, though."

"In a sec," I told him. I pressed a button and the third rocketpod went *FUSHHH* and fell apart.

"Maybe if you told me what you are trying to do," said the Boov.

The next pod just hummed and shuddered and made a beeping sound. I tried pressing some more buttons, but the console kept going *BLONG,* so I ditched it and moved on.

"Because so far," said the Boov, "you have sent empty escape pods to the roof of the Fork Museum and to the Captain Smek Memorial Balloonafish Pond in Nacho Park. I'm sending a small group of large Boov to . . . help you. So if you could just stop—"

The rocketpod that had been shuddering and beeping now started beeping faster, and then SHOOOOOOOOOOOOOOOOOOOOOOSH, the pod rocketed down the lane, through the cat flap, and out over the city.

"Aaaand now you have shot a rocketpod into the broadcasting antenna near my house. So I guess I won't be watching the debate later! Super."

"Oh," I said to myself, squinting at the new console. "That beeping . . . was a time delay. That's what I need—which button was that again?"

"Now this is strange," said the Boov on the screen. "Computer tells me that Dan Landry and his humanschild are resting in their quarters. You are someone else—aaAH!" he gasped. "You are the Squealer's human!"

I must have pressed something right, because the nearest pod started beeping like the last one. I ran around the side and threw open the hatch and climbed in as it shivered and purred. Just then I realized I was still holding the hoverbutt.

"Sorry, Funsize," I whispered. He wasn't getting it back now.

A door on the other end of the pod bay opened and a bunch of olive-green Boov rushed in just as I got the pod's hatch closed and latched and the cabin pressurized and my ears popped and I tried to strap myself in with a seat belt that was meant for an entirely different shape of person. I'd gotten it snapped more or less over my torso when a T-shaped stick popped up from the floor in front of me.

"Human!" shouted one of the green Boov as he pounded on the plastic windshield. "Exit the rocketpod!" The others heaved at the hatch, but no dice.

"You can cancel the launch sequence!" said the Boov on the screen. "Just hit command-space-three. Hurry!"

One of the green Boov raced over to the console. "Command-space-three?" he said. "In that order?"

"No, all at once!"

The beeping accelerated.

"I do not see a button that says 'command.'"

"Oh! Ha—sorry! I am thinking of my SmekBook at home. Not command. Control!"

"Never mind," said the Boov, scowling at me through the windshield as he drew his gun. "I will—"

SHOOOOOOOOOOOOOOOOOOOOOOOSH, my pod rocketed down the lane, through the cat flap, and out over the city.

NINE

I rocketed out into the night sky, the blurry shapes of smaller buildings pitching beneath me, and immediately the inside of my ship started flashing purple and making this *ENGH ENGH* sound, like that's ever helpful. If you're at the point where an escape pod even seems like a good idea in the first place, then I don't think you need a siren to tell you how your life is going.

Other Boovish ships like silver fish darted past the windshield, this way and that. I remembered that the jail where they were keeping J.Lo was in Sector 3, so I yelled that.

"Sector Three jail!" I told the rocketpod. "Sector Three!" It was about as useful as shouting "Bagel!" at a toaster. But just then I was about to crash into a tower, so I grabbed the

T-stick in front of me and yanked it to the right. I slalomed around the edge of the tower, grinding sparks, and jerked the stick to the left to avoid another. A school of little ships scattered at my approach. Finally there was a big bubble building that looked too big to avoid. It was coming up fast, so I pulled back on the stick, hard. So hard it snapped off at the base. The seat belt squeezed the air right out of me as the rocketpod slowed, getting closer to the bubble building, closer still, until—bump—my windshield bounced off a window belonging to a very startled-looking Boov on a treadmill.

The rocketpod hovered in midair, humming. I sort of waved at the Boov. The Boov gave a little wave back.

I tried to push and pull at what was left of the T-stick, but nothing worked. So instead I unfastened my belt and opened up the front of the pod. The wind howled in, smelling like tar.

At least it was night. At some point during my stay in the HighBoovperial Palace it had gotten dark, and I remembered just enough of what J.Lo had told me to know that it was going to stay that way for days. It took a long time for New Boovworld to get out from Saturn's shadow.

I balanced on the lip of the open hatch. Below me were thousands of smaller buildings, all of them glassy and round and lit up like bulbs on a marquee. Amid these were towers, antennae, bubbleship buildings with octopus hoses, a big telecloner on a low rooftop. Smokestacks and a careless fog. And, straight ahead, a Boov squinting at me from his living room. I saw the slant of a big screen. Looked like they were newscasting about tonight's presidential debate.

I made that little circular movement with my hand that means *roll down your window*, but the Boov just frowned and shrugged. "Open your window!" I shouted. "Please!" But he only stared back, blankly.

I went back for the hoverbutt and showed it to him. I tried to mime with my fingers what I wanted to do. My pod was a little too far away from the building to jump, but I hoped with the hoverbutt under me I might just make it. I thought I'd done a good job of silently explaining myself, but the Boov just winced and offered me a houseplant.

"HUMAN!" trumpeted the air, all around. "LIE DOWN ON THE FLOOR OF YOUR VEHICLE!" It buzzed in my ears and rattled the windowpane in front of me. I looked left and right and discovered that a cluster of green cruisers had snuck up on me. The Boov inside the building retreated behind an armchair.

I put my hands up, but one of them was still holding the hoverbutt. Which I figured was pretty harmless, but maybe it wasn't as commonplace as I'd assumed.

"DROP THE DEVICE!" said one of the Boov in the green cruisers. "DRRROP IT! THERE'S A GOOD BOY. DROPIT!"

But instead I put it under my butt and stepped out into nothing.

Which right away was obviously a *complete* mistake. I'd

thought the hoverbutt would let me fall as fast or slow as I wanted, but nope! I just dropped like a brick. A Styrofoam brick—low gravity and all. Still, good for a quick getaway, bad for every other conceivable reason.

The fog roiled all around. And, looking straight down as I was, the antennae passed like arrows. Like lances. Every smokestack was the barrel of a big gun. And all of it in slow motion as I fell at a rate that felt just breezy enough not to kill me, but just fast enough to get me excused from gym classes for the rest of my life. I leaned left and right, trying to steer, trying to prolong my dumb death or whatever for just another second longer. Coughing, eyes tearing against the sting of smoke and stupid failure, I didn't notice at first that a swarm of tiny bubbles was rising up to meet me.

Then the bubbles were fizzing all around me, buffeting the hoverbutt. I got so startled that I dropped it, and I watched helplessly as it was knocked off course and sailed into the darkness. Was this some kind of attack?

The bubbles kept coming, popping now against my backside and pushing feebly against my momentum. Now they came larger, big as baseballs, and larger still, a volley of volleyballs. I was actually slowing down. I looked up and saw the flashing lights of Boovcop cruisers descending after me.

Then the bubbles abruptly stopped.

I was picking up speed again. A familiar little silver bee rose up in front of my face.

"It's you!" I shouted over the rush of stale air. "That . . . billboard sign thing! Help me! Keep hitting me with bub—"

The bee swiveled around and blew a bubble the size of a washing machine, which shot out and hit me in the face.

Rather than slowing me down, it just knocked me backward. Backward, and into the open mouth of a high-rise sucktunnel.

FOOMP.

I went into a bend, whapped against the sides of the tube, and slid into a curve. And then I got barfed out the other end of the sucktunnel, proceeded to plow through a safetypillow, and touched down improbably in the center of a dark alley. No, that's not right—it wasn't a touchdown, exactly. A smackdown? Like pro wrestling, it looked both painful and fake.

I got up, shaky and panting. My seat hurt, but a glance down the alley showed me what could have been: the hoverbutt was hoverbusted, bits and stuffing everywhere. None of it my own personal bits and stuffing.

The silver bee dropped into view and hovered in front of my face.

"Hello," I said.

It pulled back and chased its tail, blowing bubbles until it formed a word.

"I *know* that one," I said. "That's 'hello.'"

The bubbles popped and the bee made a new word. I knew this one too.

YES.

"Were you . . . waiting outside the palace for me all this time?" I asked it. "How did you know it was me in the rocketpod?"

The billboard bee's antennae crackled and snapped. It juggled its bubbles and spat out more. It formed one word, then another, then another, and I had to put up my hands.

"Sorry," I said. "Sorry. I only know 'hello,' 'yes,' 'no,' and 'bathroom.'"

All the bubbles popped, or drifted away. The bee stared at me.

I thought about what J.Lo had said, about Boov moving their heads and blinking to avoid looking at these things.

"Aw," I said. "Are they not paying enough attention to you?"

NO.

Sirens were growing closer, but they sounded spread out. Like they'd lost me. There wasn't anyone else in this alley, which was open on one end.

"Do you know where Sector Three is?" I asked the bee.

NO.

"Can you . . . *spell* 'Sector Three'?"

It buzzed around, pooping bubbles, big ones and small, dot dot dot, around and around. Finally it came to rest in the center of a complex constellation. I did my best to memorize the pattern.

"I'm looking for any signs that look like that, then," I said. I looked the bee in its weird face. If that was even a face. "Thanks for helping me. Will you help me some more?"

YES.

"I'm calling you Bill. That all right?"

YES.

"Okay, Bill," I said, starting down the alley. "Let's go."

TEN

The streets of New Boovworld were all narrow and clean.
In a city where everyone took public transport and all the
big vehicles floated overhead, the strips between houses
and buildings were only as wide as a driveway and smooth,
with rounded sides. They were filled with Boov on foot.
Occasionally a scooter went humming by.

The street right ahead of me was lined with what looked
like giant gumball machines—pedestal bases with flap-
covered entrance ramps, topped by big frosted globes. Kind
of grim-looking light gray gumball machines, mind you, like
if the glass weren't frosted you'd see that all the gum was
unflavored and beige.

"Are those houses?" I whispered to Bill.

YES.

The alley where Bill and I were crouching was pretty dark, but it was also an alley with a sucktunnel at the end of it, so I wasn't expecting much privacy. Sure enough, it wasn't more than a minute before a Boov turned my way, and there wasn't any place to hide.

The Boov wore a real wiggly outfit and had one of those little winged armadillo things on a leash. He paused a few feet away from me and scowled at his pet. The armadillo noticed me right away.

"Get on with it already," the Boov told the armadillo. "Debate is starting soon."

The armadillo lifted its tail and dropped something blue out its backside. It looked like a racquetball. And bounced like a racquetball, and rolled to the side of the alley like a racquetball.

"Good boy," said the Boov, and when they turned to leave again, he saw me.

He froze. The armadillo thing beat its little wings and strained at the leash, wanting to sniff me or bite me or make me a racquetball or whatever.

I glanced at Bill, who was hovering over my shoulder, and then I gave the Boov a reluctant wave. The Boov's eyes shifted between me and the racquetball.

"I was going to pick it up," he told me. I didn't say anything. "I wasn't going to leave it," he added, and pressed his sleeve; a rubber glove snapped up over his hand. "See now?" he said, retrieving the dropping and putting it in the pocket of his coat.

"Okay," I said.

He frowned at me. "You are a human," he said. "That is weird."

Then he dragged his armadillo back out into the street.

I exhaled. "All right," I said. "That could have gone a lot worse." I looked at Bill. Bill looked at me, I think. "Still," I said, "if I keep getting noticed like that, people are going to talk. Word'll spread back to Smek, right? I need a disguise. Let me tell you what I'm thinking."

I told Bill what I was thinking. So if anyone was watching from the street about a minute later, they would have seen a five-foot-tall bubbleperson mosey out of the alley. *If* anyone had been watching from the street.

"Going out of business sale!" I said, hoping people would mistake me for a talking billboard and therefore ignore me. "Everything must go!"

But the street was empty.

Not that I noticed this right away—my face was covered in layers of tiny bubbles. I probably waddled around shouting for another minute or two. But eventually I said, "Bill? Can you uncover my eyes?" Bill, who was perched atop my head, snapped his antennae. The fizz pulled back from my face.

Yep, empty. Just a couple of odd birds on a signpost.

"What . . . happened to everyone?" I whispered. As it turned out, I got my answer a moment later when a little drone passed overhead, scaring the birds. They glided off on kite wings like flying squirrels.

"HighBoov debate starting in thirty-seven seconds!" blared the drone as it appeared over the street and disappeared behind a gumball house. "HighBoov debate starting in thirty-three seconds!"

"Huh," I said. "Well, all right! 'Bout time something went my way."

I searched the street. Opposite the side with all the gumball machines were larger buildings that I'd learn later were the Gorgwar Veterans' Clubhouse Number 17 and a condiment silo. Everywhere there were signs: some bubbly, some flat and covered with writing and pictograms. They arched over the street and jutted off every building, like fins. I remembered that this city had only been finished for a year—nobody had grown up here; nobody knew their way around. Lucky for me.

I said, "Bill? That little symbol in the corner of all the signs looks almost like 'Sector Three.' But it isn't, is it?"

NO.

"Does it say 'Sector Two'?"

YES.

I smirked and looked behind me, where I could still just see the bald curve of the HighBoovperial Palace in the distance.

"Betcha anything that's Sector One back there. I think we need to keep moving away from the palace."

Which we did, cutting directly though the narrow gap

between two gumball machines, then two more, then across a street, repeat. I still wasn't a hundred percent used to the gravity, and the occasional misstep sent me careening off one house or the next, which only made me want to run faster, which only made me bump into more houses. And despite it all I was wheezing. Bill gave me a look. Which was probably all in my head, since he didn't have a face.

"It's harder than it looks," I panted. "Maybe the air's thin here or something."

We passed a red dirt lot that was tangled with branching stalks of transparent tubing, all growing up from bell jars on the ground. Here and there a segment of tubing lit up like the whole mess was filled with fireflies. I didn't slow down enough to figure it all out. We must have passed fifty houses before I stumbled into the open of another street and found our way blocked.

An absolutely colossal building hunkered on the other side, maybe five stories tall but about a hundred wide. Like a skyscraper on its side. I guess I'd already gone native, because I thought it was weird looking for being boxy. Boxy, but not plain: it was covered in cream-colored puffy pads like it was quilted. My mom had a tissue-box cover like that; I guess it was the same kind of thing. Ramps curved up to it from every direction.

I bent at the waist, huffing. "Need a minute," I told Bill.

Strangest of all was that this building didn't have a sign on it anywhere. What it *did* have was something like a shining metal eye set in its front, and this was swiveling around and casting a spotlight all over the street. It made me anxious; I stiffened and hunched low, looking back the way I'd come, when it abruptly shifted and fixed its gaze right on me. There was a flash.

"MUSEUM OF NOISES," said a voice.

Then the eye beam resumed searching the boulevard for someone else to look at. I glanced at Bill.

"Did you hear that?"

NO.

"I think it said, 'Museum of Noises.'"

After a few seconds of giving the rest of the street the crazy eye, the beam came back to me. Flash.

"MUSEUM OF NOISES," I heard again.

"I think this is the Museum of Noises," I told Bill. I stared at it a second. "Let's cut through, if it's open." I'd really lucked out with this whole debate thing, but I knew enough about Boovish technology to not assume that the people in these gumball houses couldn't see me just because I couldn't see them.

"MUSEUM OF NOISES," the eye beam told me.

"Yeah, got it," I said.

We hustled up one of the ramps, and a door opened on its own. I stepped through and into a big oblong foyer with an information booth and doors and ramps leading everywhere. It was as empty as I'd been hoping. Quiet. A sudden tick of the foundation settling, nothing more. There was a smaller eye beam inside the entrance, and it turned to face me.

"HORK HORK HORK huk HORK HORK HORK HORK

HORK hahn hahn HORK HORK HORK HORK HORK HORK HORK HORK HORK HORK mahaign HORK huk HORK HORK HORK HORK HORK," said the eye beam. It sounded like a hundred cats all throwing up at the same time. Which is not empty talk—I heard that once.

The beam kept shooting me barf noises while I read a nearby plaque. Like in the exhibit at the palace, the signs here were written in Boovish, English, and Chinese. Not *good* English, mind you: there were some translation problems. I don't know how good or bad the Chinese was, but as languages go, I don't think it's supposed to have so many smileys.

WELCOME!NOW Human or humanslanguage-learner to the MUSEUM OF NOISES. As you saunter throughinto our many room and bodegas, electrical eyes will study your progress and beam to you a secret hullaballoo! whenfor you are humid.

A fat time for all.

At this momentnow you are enjoying the greeting-call of the Goozmen of Gooz-7. For learning more about the Goozmen, kindly visit *Flatulenture!* on Level 2.

I moved through the foyer, far enough from the plaque that the eye beam stopped horking at me. Another picked up my movement and made some kind of birdcall. I passed into the next room, and a third sent a trickling sound that made me realize suddenly that I hadn't peed in kind of a while. I was wondering what to do about that when a fourth eye beamed me a new noise that might have meant something okay to Boov but on Earth is NOT COOL.

I found a Boovish bathroom, the less said about which the better.

I stumbled through a room tiled with rubber cushions that honked and whistled when you stepped on them. And you couldn't not step on them. A bright scoreboard on one wall kept a tally of the tiles I honked and whistled, and at the end it played a sad tubaharp noise and announced, "YOU HAVE SAVED ZERO BABIES."

The next room was a gift shop.

Then there were some exhibits about other alien races J.Lo had told me about, like the Mah-pocknaph'ns, who can only speak telepathically, through living puppets. Or the Habadoo, who believe there is a name that, if ever uttered, would destroy the universe. The Habadoo all claim to know it, and they all vow to never say it out loud.

After that there was another gift shop.

Then a supercomputer that was attempting to create new noises no one had ever heard before. Then an exploration of the philosophy of noise, with questions like "If a koobish falls in the forest and no one is around to hear it, does it make a sound?" (answer: no, not really) and "What is the sound of one hand snapping?" (answer: *snap*). Then there was a statue of a Gorg that you were encouraged to make whatever noise you liked at. I passed it quietly.

Then a gift shop.

At the other end of the gift shop was a map of both the museum and a little of the surrounding area. It was here that I learned that I was just one room away from the Green Exit, and that I'd actually been in Sector 3 for a couple of exhibits now, and that visitors were discouraged from turning left out the Green Exit because that way was all work camps and a detention nub. Success! I nearly skipped through the next corridor. It opened onto a room that was wide and round and empty and tall.

I stopped abruptly. The scuff of my sneaker echoed back and forth in stiff little whispers.

High above the center of this big bell-shaped chamber was a marquee that read THE SOUND OF SPACE. It wasn't like the other exhibits. It didn't have any electronic eye, just four helmets hanging down from accordion tethers around a little center pedestal. To hear the sound of space you apparently had to put one of these helmets on.

"That's dumb," I whispered to Bill. Bill didn't have an opinion about it. I was going to have to pass these helmets to get through the room, but I wasn't tempted. "There *is* no sound in space," I told Bill.

I walked right through the center of the room. The helmets were hanging so high I wouldn't even have to duck. As I approached, each helmet dipped to meet me, but like any good city girl I avoided eye contact, didn't take a flyer, didn't stop to sign the petition or listen to the hard-luck story. They reeled up again after I'd passed.

At the Green Exit I looked back. "I don't get it," I said. I returned to the pedestal, and a helmet lowered itself, slowly, like it was worried I'd make it look foolish again. I read the English inscription on the pedestal as a cool plastic plate settled on my head and arms flexed inward to cradle my ears.

Todaynow, the Boov are nearly 8 million solar lengths from home, I read. *That is fifteen light-years. That is 142 trillion kilometers. That is 88 trillion miles.*

The helmet on my head began to hum softly.

The Boov will never again see that motherworld that made us, it continued, *and which we then treated shabbily, and did not respect, and was later then forfeit. The Museum of Noises introduces to you the Sound of Space, withto evoke the vast distance inbetween the Boovish peoples and our lost HOME.*

That was everything on the plaque. Then a pair of

blinders flapped down to cover my eyes, and the hum of the helmet fell away, and I heard nothing.

Not a recording of nothing, but actually *nothing*. The earpieces somehow canceled out the sounds of the air, and Bill's faint whirr, and distant noises I hadn't even realized I was hearing until they were suddenly gone. I heard nothing. Just my heartbeat.

"Big deal," I whispered. The sound of it was all inside my skull, and surprisingly loud. Cowed, I fell silent again and listened. I wondered what I was supposed to be thinking about. I wondered if I was supposed to remove the helmet myself or if it was a moment-of-silence kind of thing; I'd just have to ride it out until the helmet decided I'd searched my soul or whatever. My big dumb soul.

I couldn't tell if Bill was still there. I couldn't tell if any walls were still surrounding me. I might have been anywhere; I might have been home. Fell asleep with my headphones on again, I thought with a smirk.

When it came, it came without warning. I thought it was going to be a yawn. Something ordinary but unstoppable, rising up from my chest, seizing control of my mouth and eyes. Just a yawn.

Oh, I thought suddenly. I'm crying.

Inside my blinders tears pooled and escaped, drawing shameful lines down my cheeks. Like coward's war paint, I thought angrily. For J.Lo's rescue I needed *battle* cries, not the regular kind. I sat heavily on the floor, sobbing, trying to catch my breath.

I stayed there a while, and cried, and thought about vast distances.

Then the blinders flipped up, and the hum returned. I frowned and blinked into the dim light.

"THANK YOU FOR VISITING THE MUSEUM OF NOISES," said the helmet. Some flutey music played. "AS YOU LEAVE THESE VAUNTED HALLS, REMEMBER THAT NOISES ARE NOT JUST FOR MUSEUMS. YOU MAY MAKE AND LISTEN TO NOISES *ALL THROUGHOUT THE YEAR*."

I ripped the helmet off my head and threw it carelessly to the side. It retreated back up to its station.

I pressed my palms against my eyes and heard Bill whirr close.

"Something's wrong with me, Bill," I said, breathing hard and sniffling.

Bill sank down to the level of my face, looking wobbly through my tears. He swiveled around and popped a bubble against my nose.

I laughed, and sniffed, and pulled my hands across my eyes. After a minute I stood.

"Let's go get my friend and get out of town," I told Bill.

YES.

ELEVEN

The Sector 3 detention nub was a dusty little pimple of a building in the center of a ring of tall fencing. Dim lights were shining up at it from the ground. The fence wasn't going to give me any problem—I was pretty sure I'd be able to vault it with my low-gravity superpowers. Then it was about a hundred feet to the edge of the dome. I couldn't see a way in from where I was standing.

Actually, the fence looked *so* easy that it made me a little suspicious. How secure could any prison be when every Boov had a flying scooter and a gun that could make holes in anything? I squinted into the darkness and looked around, but there didn't seem to be anyone patrolling the grounds. It *was* a really small prison; J.Lo was probably the only one in there. Maybe Boov just did what they were told. Maybe Boov just stayed where they were put.

I wanted something to throw over the fence, just to see what would happen. I wished I had a racquetball.

"Oh!" I whispered to Bill. "Shoot a bubble over there!"

YES.

Bill rose to just above the level of the fence, turned, and launched a bubble inside the perimeter. It slowed once it was about thirty feet in, then drifted lazily on the ammonia-scented breeze. Nothing. No other movement inside the fence.

"Shoot another one," I said. "Shoot a big bunch."

Bill made an arrangement like a clump of grapes and snapped at it with his antennae, and it sailed over the compound like a parade balloon.

"You'd think *someone* in there would tell us to keep our bubbles out of his yard," I whispered.

"*I* would," said the Chief, who'd just joined me at the fence. "If it was my yard."

"You would, wouldn't you," I said. "You'd grab the bubbles and be all like, 'These are *my* bubbles now. You're not gettin' 'em back.'"

The Chief nodded slowly. "The Spook in there?"

"Yeah," I sighed, and stared through the bars. "I'm scared for him."

"So what's the plan?"

"No plan," I said. "Did I have a plan when I saved the whole world? Not much of one, anyway."

We were quiet a moment. Which is to say that I was quiet and the Chief was a figment of my imagination.

"I've decided you were wrong before," I told him after a while.

"Oh, good."

"It isn't just kids who go about everything wrong. It's people. I mean, I don't want to offend you or anything—"

"Ha! Since when?"

"—but you weren't exactly the most popular guy back at the casino. Or in Roswell. People thought you were . . . hard to get along with. Some people. And you are no kid, pardon me for saying so; you're like two hundred and fifty years old, so shouldn't you know by now how to make everybody like you?"

"Ah, you put your finger right on it. I could no longer give two horse apples what people think of me. That's what maturity's good for. Might be the only thing it's good for."

He paused to cough.

"The curse of *im*maturity," he said, "is that the more immature you are the more desperate you are to impress others. An' the less likely you are to do the right thing, the thing that's gonna impress 'em. So you get the teen who likes to rev his engine, drive too fast, all to show what a capable and heroic adult he is. An' all the adults he passes shake their heads an' think, 'What an idiot kid.'"

"Well," I said. "That's how I know I'm mature. I saved the

whole world, and I don't care that no one knows it. *I'm* not trying to impress anybody."

The Chief nodded, gravely. "An' I can tell how much you don't care," he said, "by the way you've mentioned it twice in the past three hours."

I squinted at him.

"Whatever," I said finally, backing up and squaring my body against the fence. "I'm going for it." I looked up at the top of the fence. I could definitely jump that.

"Don't be reckless, now."

"It's not a problem," I said, shifting my weight back and forth. "I'm a superhero here."

I dug in and leaped into a run just as a high chirp sounded and something in the sky caught my eye. It was one of those kite-shaped birds, flying overhead, flying over the fence, flying over the little dome, whereupon a big gun ratcheted up and vaporized it.

I skidded to a halt and fell over.

Inside the fence, a couple of feathers pinwheeled to the ground—they were all that was left of the bird. With a whirr, the big gun folded itself back into the top of the dome.

"Seems automatic," said the Chief. "Probably motion activated."

I crab-walked backward, heaving from the adrenaline and probably a little from a general lack of fitness. If I ever got home again, I swore, I was going to start doing jumping jacks or something. "Bubbles didn't set it off," I muttered.

"Nope."

We were quiet a while. Bill fizzed around my head.

"Well, so . . ." I began, looking at the Chief. "You're ex-military, right? What do you think I'm up against here?"

"I am *not* ex-military," said the Chief, "because I'm not real. I'm just your imagination, which you can tell by the way I'm now wearing a Hawaiian shirt."

I scowled. But he *was* wearing a Hawaiian shirt suddenly.

"I don't know anything *you* don't know," the Chief concluded. "Go ahead: ask me something you don't know."

I looked at the dome.

"Are we . . . J.Lo and me . . ." I sighed. "What's going to happen to us?"

The Chief smiled sadly.

"You're gonna be okay, kid," he said.

I frowned. "What makes you say that?"

He shrugged. "You made me say that. Suppose you must believe it."

I breathed, and nodded.

"Okay," I said, getting up. "Bill? Bubble-girl disguise, take two."

TWELVE

Something atop the prison growled. Some little servomotor whined like a dog. The motion sensors, wherever they were, ogled the yard between the jail and the fence and thought they saw a ghost.

I was dressed in bubbles. Covered head to toe in a really unflattering outfit of bubbles. It was Halloween, and this year I was going as . . . bubbles. I was trick-or-treating my first house, a big pimple with a gun that would vaporize me if it didn't like my costume.

I shuffled forward, cocooned inside a fine froth. That fine froth was inside a layer of bigger beads, then another layer like party balloons, and all of this inside one big bubble the size of a tollbooth.

Bill was in there with me. Every now and then he snapped

his antennae, sending little electric orders to the bubbles to keep them all together.

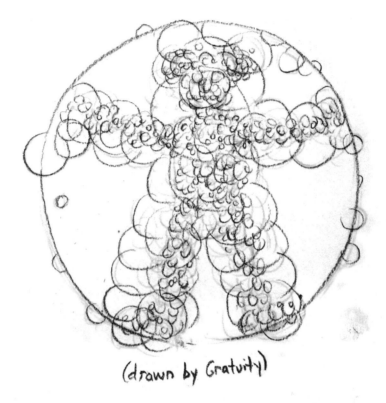

(drawn by Gratuity)

I was passing a ring of lights now, lights that shone directly on the dome ahead of me. I was always taught that you should try to draw attention *away* from a pimple this size, but whatever, different strokes.

I was about halfway there, and I *still* couldn't see a way in.

Some motion sensors won't detect you if you're not moving fast enough. Some motion sensors can't see you if you block them with clear glass. All of this came to me now, half remembered from an episode of *MythTesters*. So I minced forward in my bubble ensemble, and tried not to breathe too flamboyantly, and dared that automatic rifle not to pop suddenly out the top of the prison and erase my head.

You know what I never liked as a kid? Jack-in-the-boxes. I don't know why I mention this.

I left the lights in the yard behind, and winced at the way they cast my blurry shadow up the side of the dome.

I mean, I played with my jack-in-the-box because I didn't have a lot of toys, but I basically hated every minute of it. I'd crank it really slowly because I was too young to know that playing "Pop Goes the Weasel" slowly is what directors do to make their movies scarier. Then the clown would bang out of his clown hole, and I'd scream and whack him with a TV remote until he was locked up again.

I was still forty feet away when the dome growled another growl and the rifle cocked up and swiveled around. I froze.

It was pointed dead at me. Then with a clack it twitched to my right. Then a little too far to the left. It kept jerking its head around like a bird, an anxious mother bird who couldn't decide if I was after her egg or not.

I held my breath and did not move a muscle.

After about forty seconds of this I was turning blue, but the rifle whirred and snapped itself back into the dome again.

I exhaled, then sucked back air. When I was sure I wasn't going to pass out, I took one slow turtle step toward the jail.

CLACK, the rifle raised its head again.

And snap, Bill broke free of our bubble coat and flew off around the dome.

Coward, I thought. And my second thought was, No, that's mean—he's already been super helpful for a billboard. And then I watched the rifle swing away from me and follow Bill and I thought, Oh.

Bill was fast. The rifle swung a full circle, chasing him, and around went Bill again. And again, drawing a ring of bubbles behind him, tracing and retracing an O above my head.

I surged toward the dome, leaving my disguise behind me like a cartoon cloud. I heard the rifle seize up, swing back the other way. We had it good and confused now, and it fired over my head, erasing the bubbles and creating a good-sized divot in the yard. I reached the edge of the dome and leaped, landing on my hands and knees about halfway up and scrambling the rest of the way, then ducking as the rifle came around again. I stood up behind its butt end and scrambled this way and that to stay behind the butt end as it swiveled back and forth.

I said "butt end" a couple of times. Pardon my language.

Anyway, the rifle looked like it might have Bill in its

sights, so I leaped on top, trying to wrestle it in a safer direction. Instead it spun so fast it threw me clear.

"YeeeeEEEEE!" I shrieked, and skidded a few feet down the side of the dome. I raised my head and saw the rifle turning to give me a good look up its barrel again, so I pushed off with my legs as hard as I could. The rifle lit up again and fired, and I heard a loud *BWOMP* behind me.

Now I was just crouching under the rifle's chin. It spun and spun but couldn't find me anymore. I glanced back and saw that the dome had a small smoking dent where I'd been sitting a moment before. A dent, but no hole. So there—this prison was made from some reinforced material that even the eraser guns couldn't breach.

Up high like this, I could see that the dome was connected by a covered tunnel to a smaller dome near the fence on the opposite side. But more importantly, there was a narrow hole in the tippy-top of the dome where I was crouching—a missing jigsaw piece the exact size and shape of a collapsible rifle. It was small—way too narrow to fit a Boov. But a thirteen-year-old who hadn't had anything to eat for the past twenty-four hours?

I squinted down through the gap. It was kind of dark in there, but it looked like a hallway. Possibly an empty hallway. I kicked my legs in, dangled them down, pushed my fat belly through, then got stuck at the shoulders.

The rifle turned and turned.

Bill appeared and landed on my head. I couldn't see him anymore, but I felt him like a big barrette in my hair.

"Bill!" I said. "Thank God, pardon my language. You're a brave little billboard."

I heard Bill spell something that I probably wouldn't have been able to read anyway.

"I'm stuck, Bill," I said, as the frame of the rifle's housing cut into my armpits. "Ow. Maybe you could squirt some bubbles down here and butter me up a little?"

The rifle had grown still.

"Hey," I said. "I just thought of something. If the gun doesn't have anything to shoot at anymore, does that mean it's going to—"

The gun collapsed on top of my head and knocked me like a square peg through the gap.

I crumpled to the hallway below. Groaning, I clutched my head and opened my eyes. Bill was making tipsy figure eights above me.

"Ugh," I said. "You okay, Bill?"

Bill bumped into my face.

I tried to rise, missed, tried again. As I got to my feet, one of the walls of the corridor flickered with light.

And in the light was J.Lo.

"J.Lo!" I cheered. "Finally! Are you okay?"

J.Lo looked like he answered, but I couldn't hear it. He was in a cell, the only cell in this corridor, and it was behind a wall of thick glass. The other three walls were close, and made from a very serious-looking honeycomb of black metal. He had a little sleeping chair and a chair for something I preferred not to think about, and in an upper corner of the cell was a screen, silently playing the presidential debate. The TV camera fixed on Smek, and now Sandhandler, and I thought, Wow, it really *is* mandatory.

J.Lo looked like he was shouting something new, but I still couldn't hear. Then he stopped and sighed. He pressed his hands to the glass. He smiled at me.

I smiled back. "You can hear me?" I asked.

He nodded.

"And I can't hear you because of some gadget, right? Some stupid noise-canceling thing that's supposed to make you think about the emptiness of space and feel all bad about yourself?"

J.Lo frowned and mouthed, *What?*

"Forget it," I said. "Your voice is okay?"

He nodded again, and pointed at the bluzzer doing loop-de-loops by my ear.

"Oh!" I said. "J.Lo, this is William Board. His friends call him Bill. Bill, J.Lo."

J.Lo waved. Bill tried to spell something, but all that came out his backside was a glob of foam.

J.Lo pointed to my right, and then at his mouth, and back to the right again. Next to the glass was a big panel of knobs and buttons. So I pressed and switched and turned and mashed everything like the kind of little kid who thinks a soda machine will give him a free Coke if he just wants it badly enough. And it kind of did give me a free Coke—that is, a can of *something* shot from a slot inside the cell and hit J.Lo on the back of the head. And a koobish dropped in from the ceiling, and the lights above J.Lo changed colors a few times, and a dozen robot arms flexed out from the walls and punched him all over with tiny mittens.

"Sorry!" I said. "Sorry!" I tried to put all the buttons and switches back how they'd been. The lights were stuck on pink, but the arms ratcheted back into the walls. J.Lo rose from the floor, wearily.

The koobish minced around the cell, and noticed the glass partition, and walked into it.

"Okay," I said, squaring myself against the wall. "Stand back. I'm, like, super strong on this planet, right? Maybe I can break it." J.Lo hopped to the rear of the cell. Even the koobish stepped back—leaving a greasy, koobish-shaped print—and watched me throw a punch and crack my knuckles against the glass.

I tried not to cry in front of J.Lo. But I bent over and pressed my hand into my mouth.

"Ow."

The koobish was smooshing its face around on the glass. J.Lo took a bite out of its rump before pushing it aside.

132

Then he opened his huge mouth wide and huffed on the glass, tracing a fingertip across it before the fog faded. He still wasn't great with written English—if you ever need your lemonade stand to look adorably stupid, you'll want J.Lo to paint the signs. So when the fog read

I figured I knew roughly what he was talking about. I didn't.

"Sell my phone?" I said. "Like for bail money? But I didn't even bring it, remember? You said it wouldn't work here."

J.Lo stared for a moment with a deflating head before brightening and fogging up the glass again.

I pressed my palms against the window. "I. Didn't. Bring. It. I thought you could hear me on that side. I don't have a cell pho—"

J.Lo was drumming on his face in frustration. Then he put a finger up like he was playing charades and mimed that he was rattling invisible bars.

"Jail?" I asked, and when he nodded I got it. "Oh! *Jail* cell phone!" I looked at the panel again. "One of these things is a phone?"

J.Lo muttered silently to himself, then breathed on the glass again and drew a word in Boovish:

Which I guess meant "mute," because I found a button labeled just like that and pushed it, and suddenly J.Lo was muttering to himself in high-def sound that rattled like a low-flying airplane straight through the wall behind me.

"... 'CAUSE IF YOU HAD ONLY BEEN STUDYING THE BEGINNING BOOVISH FLASHEDCARDS LIKE YOU PROMISED THEN YOU COULD READ THE BUTTONS YOURSELFOH HELLO IS THE PHONE ON NOW?"

I found the volume and turned it down. On the TV Ponch Sandhandler was saying, "My opponent will tell you it takes a strong leader to maintain a well-ordered society."

I glanced at it, and you could see that Smek *had* planned

to say that, because he crossed something out on his speech. Sandhandler continued:

> But I tell you that a well-ordered society that never changes doesn't *need* a strong leader. What has the house of Smek done for *you* lately?

I tried to ignore the TV. I'm one of those people at restaurants who can't stop watching the hockey game on the set behind you, even though I don't care about hockey. It's a problem.

"How are you feeling?" I asked J.Lo.

"Relieved. The TV just reported that you died again."

"Again?"

"Second time today."

> Ladies and gentlemen and ladygentlemen and gentleladies and gentlementlemen and mentlegentladies and gentlemenmenmenmen: I say that you good people take care of *yourselves*. You maintain your own society! But we are like clocks, forever going around and around and never moving forward!

"Are you watching the television?" asked J.Lo.

"Sorry," I said.

"I guess I had thought that we were having a friendship moment," J.Lo added.

"We were. I'm just expecting something to happen. At the debate. Something I overheard earlier."

"Well, you can let me know whento it comes. I will just relax here inside my filthy prison."

"No, seriously," I said. "I'm sorry. Now how do I get you out?"

"There is there a combination lock on the other side: five variables, each with ten possible values."

"Yes! Okay!" I said, and I started blindly turning the digits, trying combinations.

"Now," said J.Lo: "with only five variabilities and ten possibles we can determines that there are merely one hundred thousand combinations, so that if you keep trying one every second it will only take . . . on average . . . thirteen hours."

I paused. "Thirteen *hours*?"

"Well, fourteen. I rounded downward so you would not get discouraged."

We stared at each other, uselessly. On the TV, Sandhandler was saying

> Five hundred years ago we were excited about
> the change from lighter-than-air ships to
> heavier-than-air ships. The ships we enjoy
> today are still very similar to those earliest designs.

Do you know what the humans were excited about five hundred years ago? Chimneys.

The crowd gasped.

"Chimneys!" Sandhandler said again. "Andyetnow look how far they have come! While we are as stagnant as the pond that bears Smek's name in Nacho Park!"

J.Lo said, "Are you watching the—"

"No. No, I was just thinking. I'll have to look around the rest of the prison," I said. "Right?" There was a door at one end of this corridor. It probably led to that covered tunnel and the smaller dome that I'd seen earlier. Probably some other Boov, too. "Maybe someone will have the combination written down . . . somewhere."

I think the impossibleness of what I'd been trying settled in on us both. Even Bill's loop-de-loops had a little less verve. Only the koobish was happy, galumphing around the cell with a bite out of its butt.

On the TV, Smek said:

My jerk opponent thinks my leadership has not been forward-thrusting and dynamic! He says that you, the good Boovish people, have stagnated! How dare he do this? Also, do not stagnant ponds also change?

A stagnant pond grows things. Unexpected things!
Under the quiet surface a thousand million bacteria are
hustling and bustling! You, my people, are like bacteria!

This wasn't going over super well with the crowd.

"You need to find somebody who will be on your side,
Tip," said J.Lo. "Someones who will listen, and get you safely
home again. Maybies this Sandhandler."

"Actually, there might be someone else on New
Boovworld who can help," I told him.

"Yes? Whonow?"

Well, let me introduce you to a man who does
not think Ponch Sandhandler should be the new
HighBoov. Ladies and gentlemen and ladygentlemen
and gentleladies and gentlementlemen and
mentlegentladies and gentlemenmenmenmen:
I give you the hero of Earth, Dan Landry!

"Him," I said.

"Unexpected turn of events from Captain Smek," said
a newscaster, as Landry took the stage. "Are candidates
allowed to have special guests during the debate, Bish?"

"No idea, Chad," said the other newscaster. "But the
crowd here has gone wild for the human whom many Boov
affectionately call 'not completely useless.'"

"Yes!" said J.Lo. "You will find Dan Landry and go back to Earth with him. Then Landry will call the president of the United States, and *he*—"

J.Lo was interrupted by a low rumble that came from beyond the door at the end of the hall. A distant rumble, but a big one that you could feel in your feet, up your legs, in the pit of your stomach.

"What was—"

Another noise, closer. A loud bang of some kind. Then the sound of a whole room collapsing. And I had nowhere to go. I'd lost the hoverbutt, so I couldn't get out the way I'd come in, and all the while the noises got louder and nearer to the hallway's only door.

> "Thank you!" said Dan Landry. "Thank you all! It is an honor to visit your fine new home."

We were quiet, watching the door. Even the koobish watched. Then footsteps, Boovish footsteps, and suddenly a hole appeared in the hallway door.

The remains of the door fell clattering to the floor, and we all jumped. And through the hole stepped a masked Boov with a really big gun. Which he then pointed at me.

He wore a rubber uniform, the kind of suit J.Lo used to wear. But every one of those suits *I'd* ever seen came in the same five colors, and this one was uniquely black.

Black all over, the matte black of stealth bombers and secret conspiracies. His mask was black too, with dark goggles and a skeletal grille over the mouth.

I figured I was dead, but the masked Boov hesitated. He lowered his gun.

"You," he said with a buzzing, electronic voice.

> Captain Smek is telling the truth, you know, when he says that I don't think Ponch Sandhandler should be president. I don't. Let me tell you a little about the guy who *should*.

I squinted at the mystery Boov. When someone knows me and I don't remember them, I usually try to fake it. "Uh, hey!" I said. "Good to see you again—"

His gun was all black too, unlike any Boov gun I'd ever seen, with a scribble of tubes and triggers and a wide horn on the business end. If Batman had decided to avenge his dead parents mostly through trombone lessons, he might have owned an instrument like this. The masked Boov raised it again, but not at me—at J.Lo.

"DEATH TO THE DESTROYER OF WORLDS!" said the Boov, and I leaped to tackle him as he fired. As usual, I didn't compensate for the weird gravity, but I still managed to kick him in the face as I passed overhead. I landed on my side in the outer room, which was full of holes and hissing pipes and flickering lights. I recovered and dashed back into the hall just in time to grab at the masked Boov's gun and spoil another shot. Bill was bluzzing around, trying to make bubbles, but there was something wrong with him.

> The next leader of New Boovworld will be a
> strong man. A *courageous* man. A man who did
> what no other leader could do.

There were two big holes in the glass partition of J.Lo's cell now, and a koobish that was missing its back legs. J.Lo tried to hide behind the toilet.

"Maa," said the koobish.

"Gratuity!" buzzed the masked Boov as we grappled over his gun. "Do not fight me! It must be done!"

I have to admit he startled me a little, using my name like that. It gave him an opening, and he wrenched the trombone rifle away from me and turned to fire again. I rammed him in the back and he shot a hole in the ceiling before tumbling down the hallway.

I could see right out to the open sky. *This* gun didn't have any problem shooting through the prison walls.

I darted through one of the holes in the glass. Bill followed, and when the masked Boov got to his feet, he found me shielding J.Lo with my body.

A new kind of leader for a new time.

Ladies and gentlemen and . . . you know,

the rest of you . . .

"Don't!" said J.Lo, trying to push me aside. "You mustnot! He will kill us both!"

"No, I . . ." I stammered. "I think I know who he is. He likes me. I don't think he'll—"

"I am sorry, Gratuity," said the masked Boov in his creepy voice, and he steadied his rifle.

. . . tonight I officially announce my candidacy for

president of New Boovworld!

I grabbed J.Lo and launched us both off the toilet seat as the masked Boov fired. Like with any other Boov gun, there was no noise, no light. So I'd find out later that I'd lost a shoelace but we'd otherwise dodged the worst of it. And now there was a gaping hole in the back wall of the prison. Fresh air breezed in from outside, or whatever passed for fresh air on New Boovworld.

Every blast of that trombone rifle knocked the masked Boov back a bit, but in a moment he had it aimed again. J.Lo grabbed the can I'd hit him with earlier and chucked it. We made a break for it, reaching the fresh exit just as the can lodged in the horn of the rifle and the masked Boov pushed the trigger and, with a honking sound, the whole barrel of it curled up and disintegrated.

(drawn by Gratuity)

"Holy cow, J.Lo!" I said as he and Bill and I ran away from the prison. "Good arm!"

"YOU WILL NOT TO ESCAPE ME!" the other Boov bellowed behind us. "YOU WILL BE STOPPED!"

J.Lo smiled a wincey smile. "I was aiming for his head," he admitted.

THIRTEEN

We crouched in doorways. We scurried like rats through
alleys. Hiding places were scarce in a city where they thought
the translucent bubble was the absolute best shape for
everything.

"At least it is night," said J.Lo. "Ifto it was bright outside,
everybodies would have their house globes unfrosted."

I saw what he meant. All those fishbowls were fogged up
so people couldn't see in from the street. Like drapes.

Too bad J.Lo had lost his own personal foggy fishbowl.
They'd taken his helmet away when they arrested him. He
was running around with his hands in front of his eyes so he
wouldn't be recognized as a notorious criminal, but he just
looked like a notorious criminal who runs into a lot of poles.

"My head feels weird," I said, breathing hard.

J.Lo lowered his arms for a second and checked it. "Do you remembers when you were trying to decide if you are too old for your hair spongeys?" he said.

I cringed. "Yeeah . . ."

"A mysterious assassin decided it for you."

I patted at my hair. I was missing half an Afro puff. "Shoot."

Bill putted around, *putt putt putt.*

"We gotta get you a new helmet," I added. "If we had a sheet, we could make people think I'm a Boov. It'd be the ghost costume again, but in reverse."

J.Lo leaned against a pole he'd just run into. "You would be a very tall Boov," he said.

"But if I . . ." I said, trying to make it work in my head. "If I still had that hoverbutt, I could sit down and just, you know, scoot along. That would make me shorter. If I wore a helmet and a sheet and no one looked too closely—"

"If you still had that what?" asked J.Lo, pushing himself upright to look at me.

"The hoverbutt. It was this little floaty thing that Funsize gave me."

"Funsize."

"Yeah. Whatever, I don't know what it's called in Boovish."

"It is not called 'hoverbutt,' I am telling you that." He chortled. "Hoverbutt."

"Oh, come *on*—how is that any more ridiculous than

anything else the Boov say? You people give everything a funny name. You're the Australians of the galaxy."

"I am rubber but you are blue. Whatevers you are saying bounces off of me and I do not remembers the rest."

"Maybe this is a dumb question," I said, "but is there any way we could get up to long-term parking? We need to get back to Slushious."

"You are right. It is a dumb question."

"Thanks."

"We would then need a car to get to the car. I would have to build one." J.Lo thought a moment. "Or maybies build a weapon for hijacking one."

I didn't like the sound of that.

"Either which way, I need a workshop," said J.Lo. "I am needing a place with parts, where I can build something to help us. Back on *Old* Boovworld there was a big field near Bigfield where we puts broken things: kroosers, bubbleships, outdated telecloners."

I nodded. "I've been to a place like that," I said.

* * *

The Chief had taken me there. Shortly after the Boov left Earth, back when we were still living in the casino just outside Tucson.

"Where are we going again?" I asked him. He was driving us in his pickup around the south side of the city, toward the air force base. Lincoln sat between us like a chaperone, his hamburger-sized paws on the dash.

"Junkyard," the Chief answered.

I was quiet for a couple exits.

"I'll bet you didn't date much when you were younger, did you?" I asked.

"You'll like it," he said. "Trust me."

When it came into view, I knew he was right.

"The Three Hundred Ninth Aerospace Maintenance and Regeneration Group," he announced. "Commonly known as the Boneyard."

It was this vast dirt parking lot filled with airplanes, and not just airplanes: it was a rest home for every kind of plane and helicopter you could think of. A dry ocean. Big bombers like beached whales. Monster-movie dragonflies and prehistoric predators with teeth painted right onto their nose cones. Some decrepit, or picked clean—just a rib cage in the sun. Others protected by muzzles and blindfolds of white vinyl.

"I guess that's pretty cool," I whispered.

I don't think we were supposed to be able to walk around in it like we did, but back in those days there was a lot of stuff that people forgot to keep an eye on. I hadn't realized we were looking for anything in particular until the Chief stopped by a little single-seat airplane with bent wings and a propeller.

"Here it is," he said. "The F-4-U Corsair. Flew an early prototype in World War Two."

It looked like nothing so much as a huge model kit. It looked pretty great, actually—even if it was falling apart.

The Chief patted its blunt nose. "I was part of a crack team of young volunteers in the days before we were officially in the war. The Teen Platoon, they called us."

"That's a cute name."

"Cute!" The Chief blew a raspberry. "We saved the president! Fought saboteurs! There was me, Smoky, Zero, Sikh and Destroy, this little midget guy—we never did learn his real name . . ."

I stared at him a moment. It sounded like a comic book. I said, "Chief? Did any of that really happen?"

He frowned at the Corsair. "Doesn't sound too likely, does it."

"I mean, I've never heard about any of this, and I watch a lot of History Channel."

Lincoln came back from wherever he'd been exploring, and licked the Chief's hand, and took off again.

"Weren't allowed to talk about it," the Chief said. "Classified. Shouldn't even be telling you." After this he started walking, so I fell in behind him.

"I'm glad you are," I said. "Telling me. We're both secret heroes! We should have masks and a lair."

He was quiet for a bit. "I worry about you," he said finally.

"That's sweet. I worry about you too."

"No, I mean . . . it's a punishing life, living with secrets. You're gonna have a weird, crazy-making road ahead if you think the world owes you but you won't tell 'em why. Or even if you did tell 'em—ours is a nation that likes to forget."

"So I'll have a hard life. Lots of people have hard lives."

"Sure, an' not all of 'em can handle it with grace an' dignity like I did."

I looked at him flatly. "Chief," I said. "Back in Roswell you were known mostly for living in a junkyard and shouting at tourists."

He nodded. "Do you remember my spaceship?"

Of course I did. Back in New Mexico the Chief had had a genuine Boovish rocketpod. An old experimental model that had crashed there in 1947 with only a koobish riding inside. He'd kept it in his basement, covered in papier-mâché and tinfoil with a TV antenna on top. Like a flying saucer a little kid would make. If anyone came looking for the famous

Roswell UFO, he'd just happily show it to them and they'd go away again.

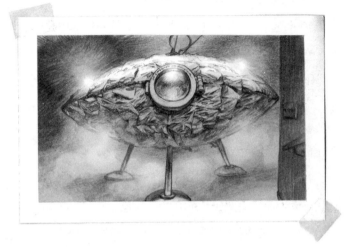

"All that tinfoil kept it safe," said the Chief. "All those years. And my crazy Indian act kept me sane—same thing. That make any sense?"

"Nope," I told him. But I took his hand anyway.

"Yeah," he said. "Didn't sound like it was gonna."

* * *

"Are you okaynow?" asked J.Lo. "You have gone spacey. We have to keep to moving."

I nodded. "I don't know about any big fields," I said, "but I do know a place with a lot of junk."

"Ohyes?"

As we crept and crawled along beneath bubble buildings and windowsills, I filled J.Lo in on all the stuff that had happened to me since we were separated.

"We should go visit this Funsize!" said J.Lo. "Sounds like he would have himself some quality garbages."

"Yeah, except he's the guy who just tried to kill us."

J.Lo flinched. "Is it true? Whynow?"

I shook my head. "He blames you for losing him his job," I said. "It was a pretty weak argument, honestly. But you heard that guy back at the jail. He *knew* me. He called me Gratuity. And they both have similar tastes in masks."

"Wellthen. Somesplace else. Somesplace with parts so to I can build something."

"To help us get home," I agreed, "where we can send a message to all the Boov and tell them what you did."

J.Lo wiggled his fingers. "Or . . ." he said. "*Or*, we finds a way for sending the message first, *then* leave."

We looked at each other. I *really* really wanted to get home.

"You don't think we should just try to escape as fast as possible?"

"But seenow? If first we send a message, then the escaping will be easier. Because then no Boov will stop us."

"If they believe you, that is."

"If they believes me, yes."

I sighed. I ached all over just to go back to Earth and hit the redo button and pretend this whole trip had never happened. It was an iffy plan, and it required my mom to get amnesia for some reason, but wasn't mine a nation that forgets? I remembered somebody telling me that at some point.

"The Chief did all this crazy stuff in World War Two," I told J.Lo. "It was all classified, so when he came out of the army, nobody knew he was a hero; they just thought he was some random Indian with a shoplifting arrest on his record from when he was eighteen." I winced. "I don't even think he wanted credit for the good stuff anymore, at the end. I think he just wanted to be forgiven for everything else."

"Yes," said J.Lo. "Forgiven." He smiled sadly.

"Okay," I said. "Message first."

We heard a distant shout then. So we ducked and squeezed ourselves into the black shadow beneath a ramp.

"Oranges!" came the shout again, getting closer. "Fancy oranges!"

"I guess we're lucky there haven't been *more* people on the streets," I whispered. "That part of town we were in earlier was hopping."

"Eh, that was the city hub," J.Lo whispered back. "Thishere is more of a huburb."

"'Suburb,'" I corrected.

J.Lo fidgeted. "Pretty sure it is 'huburb,'" he said.

"Oranges here!" the voice shouted, closer.

It was all little bubble houses up and down this alley, and dim floating lamps, and a sucktunnel opening a few doors down. After another minute, a Boov pulling a hoverwagon passed.

We sat there shivering as a door opened *right above us* and someone came tramping down the ramp.

"I will pay you for sixteen oranges!" said this new Boov.

The orange salesman paused near the sucktunnel and they did business. Sixteen oranges were parceled out from beneath the wagon's lid, and then the buyer trotted back up the ramp, carrying them in a plastic basket.

After the Boov was back inside and the orange vendor had turned to leave, I whispered, "Man, we're lucky neither one of them saw—"

J.Lo pushed me out into the light of the alley.

"Quickly!" he said. "Go pretend to buy oranges. Your face was never onto the television!"

I hesitated, then started jogging toward the vendor. "Great," I muttered through my teeth. "A *J.Lo* plan. Hey! Hello?" I added, louder. "I wanna buy some oranges too."

He'd barely gotten his hovercart going before he stopped again and turned to look at me in wonder. Didn't get a lot of human customers, I suppose.

"Ahnow," he said. "This is a surprise. Am I speaking to the famous Earthman Dan Landry?"

"In the flesh!" I said as I came to a stop, puffing. You'd think with all the fleeing I did that I'd be in better shape.

"And you have a bluzzer!" he added. "For some reason."

I glanced up to my left and found Bill swaying beside my ruined Afro puff.

"A homing bluzzer," I agreed. "They gave it to me so I wouldn't get lost."

"Ahyes. And how many oranges can I get you, Earthma—" he started to ask, but then there was an approaching patter and J.Lo galloped up and pushed the orange vendor into the sucktunnel and *FOOMP* he was gone.

"Oh," I said. As J.Lo plans went, that was pretty cut-and-dry.

"Fast now!" J.Lo shouted. "Before he returns!" He popped the lid off the cart, emptied all but maybe a dozen oranges out of it, climbed inside, and pulled the lid back over him as I finally caught on. I grabbed the hovercart's handle and ran off with it into the fog.

FOURTEEN

After hours of pulling the cart through the dark alleys,
accidentally selling two oranges, and getting as far as
possible away from our jailbreak, we needed a rest.

"We have *got* to get out of the open," I told him when
we had an alley to ourselves for a moment. "Don't you think?
Don't you think they've probably told everyone to be on the
lookout for humans by now?"

"Lookthere!" he said, peeking through a gap in the lid.
"Try that door!"

It was a typical little bubble house, up a ramp about ten
feet from the street, with a wriggling heap of koobish out
front. J.Lo explained that the owner must get regular koobish
delivery, but since the koobish were piling up on the doorstep,
he probably wasn't home. I dragged us both up the ramp,

thinking it couldn't possibly be as easy as just trying the door, but then we did and it was. Apparently nobody locks their homes on New Boovworld.

So I finally got a shower and a full night's sleep.

I dreamed my mom was running for Mom. She'd thought it was a lifetime appointment, like a Supreme Court justice, but now elections were coming up and she had competition. I never could get a good look at this competitor. Like, they'd show her on TV, but the camera was always blurry, or else my eyes were. And all I'd make out was a shape, a Bigfoot, a Loch Ness Monster.

Mom and I were staying up all night making campaign posters with student council–quality slogans like *MOM upside-down is WOW!* and *Mom for Mom: it Just Makes ¢ents,* whatever that meant. Soon I couldn't read the sign I was making at all. Which got me anxious, because I knew they were expecting me to read it in front of everybody, and then it turned into one of those stage-fright dreams where I was up at the podium and didn't know what was expected of me.

Silence in the audience. Silence plus a cough, which was worse. And my mom standing at the other podium, across the stage from me, mouthing the word *Why?* with the strangest look on her face. . . .

And that was what I woke to. On the floor I woke, with a foam pillow under my head and a koobish sniffing my hair.

I rolled over and looked up at the koobish. Its walleyed

oven-mitt face stared back at me. "Morning," I said.

"Maa-ah."

The koobish moved on—and now I had an unobstructed view of the bedroom mirror, and of the stupid decision I'd made about my hair when I was tired.

In my sleep I'd forgotten that I'd lost an Afro puff when that masked Boov had shot at us. Where once I'd had a little topiary ball, now I had a radar dish. So after my shower I'd asked J.Lo to find me a scissors or something to even it out, and consequently I had two radar dishes.

But he'd used those scissors to get my collar off, too, so that felt good. He took it apart and stripped the wires out of it, mumbling something like, "For to magnetizing the humblescrews." At the time I was too busy falling asleep to care.

I got up and looked around the bubble house.

It was like this: The outer walls were a big fishbowl that cycled air in and out *and* filtered it *and* made it room temperature. The innermost layer of the glass was also bioluminescent—did I spell that right? It was glowy. It did this neat trick where it shone, facing in, so that the rooms all had this nice Christmas-light glow but people outside could only see frosty brightness. J.Lo told me that if you stared at any point on the wall long enough, it turned transparent to let you see outside, so I tried not to do that.

Inside the fishbowl were a number of ramped platforms and a couple of smaller bubbles for the bedroom and bathroom. The shower was an antigravity capsule in which you got sprayed by a thousand nozzles in every direction and was more fun than a ride at Happy Mouse Kingdom.

I descended the ramp from the bedroom to find J.Lo and about a half dozen koobish. The koobish were just milling about, nuzzling things. They were making the room smell like bleach.

"You are up!" J.Lo said with a smile. A big curved screen was silently playing a cooking show behind him. This screen was linked by silver tubes to a liver-shaped plastic box, which J.Lo had disassembled on a blanket in front of him.

"Hey," I said. "You get any sleep? Have you been watching the news?"

"A little sleep. I had to been watching the news, but it was alls same-o same-old. Here."

He tapped at something inside the box, and the screen flipped through a couple more cooking shows before settling on a news station. Smek was holding a press conference in that same big office of his we'd visited earlier. J.Lo turned up the sound.

J.Lo turned the sound down. "I can begin it over from the start, if you like," he said.

"That's okay," I said. "Where's Bill?"

At the sound of his name the little bluzzer bluzzed into the room.

HELLO.

"Hey, Bill! You look better!"

YES.

"I could to unpoke some of his dings and swab out his foozpipe," said J.Lo.

"I was going to recommend that," I said. "Is it . . . is it normal for him to be like this? Are billboard bluzzers usually this smart and helpful?"

NO.

"Not usualies," J.Lo agreed. "But this sort of thing can sometimes to happen. If a robot is for too long frustrated at its job."

Bill was slaloming in and out of koobish's ears. They tried to nip at him as he passed.

"I don't understand that," I admitted. "Frustrated?"

J.Lo set down the pieces he was fiddling with. "Yes. Aslike . . . a robot who always wants to do, but it cannot do. When we wants to do something but cannot, that is when we think. When our consciousness awakes up and stretches its arms. That is when we imagine, and plan, and dream about the undone thing. Ignored for too long and not able to show anyBoov his message,

Bill developed a bug. Some bad code. A . . . *glitch.*"

I felt weird talking about Bill right in front of him like this. After he zoomed up the ramp to the bedroom, I said, "A glitch? Bill can *think.* Like he's *alive.* He might be as smart as a person—that's not a glitch."

J.Lo gave me a sad look. "Peoples *are* glitches," he said.

He returned to his work. "Their worlds do not want them," he continued. "A fox? It knows how to be a fox. Any koobish is the number one expert at being a koobish. But peoples? Boov and humans and Gorg and Habadoo and suchlike? We are the only ones who don't know how to be. Who do not know the right things to do."

I didn't know what to do or say for a minute, so I sat down next to the blanket. As the koobish shifted around, I saw more things—appliances, computers, and whatnot—all with their cases opened and their insides disassembled.

"So," I said. "Are we sure the Boov who lives here isn't coming home soon?"

"Pretty sure. I found his itinerary in his message box: Mr. M'Pillowclock is spending two Earth weeks camping on Mars with his work group. He just forgot to cancel his koobish delivery."

"And so you're taking all his stuff apart for him . . . why?"

J.Lo grinned. "Just working onto a couple of projects. Do you remembers when I mentioned about to making a time machine?"

My insides felt ten times heavier. "You're making a *time machine*?"

"Eh. I am only playing around."

I looked around at all the parts. "So it's possible? Time travel?"

"To the future?" said J.Lo. "Yes. Always. We do it alls the time, in miniature ways. But to the past? Also yes. But harder. Takes a crazy lot of power. Anyone who has ever traveled in a faster-than-light starship has traveled backward in time a little. And I believe such a person has then a Time River that flows through alls their past selves. Such a person could swim against the current of that river, and revisit events that have already beforenow happened to them. But it takes a buffaload of energy to swim against the current."

"I keep meaning to talk to you about that word of yours," I said. "'Buffaload.' The term is 'buttload,' pardon my language. There's no such word as 'buffaload.'"

"I invented it! It means a buffalo's load."

"Whatever—so could I go back in time?" I asked, because maybe I could visit the past and talk both of us out of coming here to New Boovworld in the first place.

"No, you could not," J.Lo said with an apologetic smile. "You have not a Time River, because you have never traveled faster than light."

"Not even on the trip from Earth?"

"Not even for a moment, no."

We stared at each other for a bit; then he shrugged and went back to his tinkering. One of the taller koobish walked over to where I was sitting and didn't stop until he was standing directly over me like a canopy bed.

"J.Lo," I said, "you can't go back in time."

"Probablies not. I mean, I think the theory is good, but where would I get so much energies?"

"Mah!" the koobish agreed. I shoved it away. It made a noise like *fuff* and wandered off.

"No," I said. "I mean . . . you *can't*. If you go back and make it so you never sent the signal, then . . . then you and I would probably never have met! And it was only together that we figured out how to defeat the Gorg!"

J.Lo looked up. "But without the signal there would have been no Gorg to defeat."

"Maybe. Or maybe they would have found you guys again anyway."

J.Lo nodded. "Or maybies they *never* would have found us guys again."

After I was rough with that one koobish, all the others seemed to make a point of bumping into me.

"Anyways," said J.Lo. "You will like this big-time." He held up a springy set of plastic teeth, like a big hair clip. "Waveform device!"

"Waveform device!" I cheered as a koobish head-butted me.

"Yes!" said J.Lo.

"I don't know what that is!" I said.

"Ah. Well. I made it fromto Mister M'Pillowclock's microwave, and some other things. When I clamp it on to these tubes, I will be able to broadcast a message. Break into all the live video feeds, probablies. And send my message into everyBoov's message box, alls at the same time."

"Hm," I said. Usually in stories when someone interrupts all the TV broadcasts it's to threaten to poison the reservoir or something. "What are you going to tell everyone?"

"I'll to explain about the antenna-farm mistake, and figuring out about cloning and teleporting, and sending the Gorg packing with all those cats. Captain Smek will not be able to silence me if everyone knows."

So that's what we did. The little liver-shaped box he'd been playing with had a tiny camera and a microphone, like a laptop. J.Lo clamped the waveform dealie on the cables, and suddenly there was his face on the TV. He flipped the channels and they all showed his face, plus the occasional koobish wandering through the background.

And he told them his story. Our story. In his own language he told all of New Boovworld our story, and he even waved me over to share the camera with him. I think I mostly fidgeted and nodded from time to time. I didn't know what to do with my hands. After a bit Bill flew into the frame and settled lightly on my head.

J.Lo was silent a moment. It made me uncomfortable, so I said, "Yeah," and then a koobish ran into me.

"That is all," J.Lo finished, and he unclipped the waveform device.

Immediately the television switched back to its regular programming. A Boov chef holding a knife and a fish said, "Are we back? What was that?"

In the bubble house I smiled at J.Lo. "You did really good," I said.

"I sent it also to Tipmom's e-mail," he said, grinning. "It will take maybe an hour to get there, but—"

I leaned over and hugged him. The koobish came up from all sides and smooshed us.

FIFTEEN

I was sipping a milk shake that J.Lo had made me with Mister M'Pillowclock's telecloner. I was too hungry to care where it came from. J.Lo filled a bag with some of the gadgets he was working on, left a note of apology to Mister M'Pillowclock, and went up to the bedroom to arrange for a shuttle to pick us up and take us back to Slushious. Nothing to do but go for it and see what happens, we agreed.

A second presidential debate was about to start. On the debate stage were three podiums. Smek and Landry stood unhappily behind two of them. On the third was Smek's parrot. Sandhandler's party had panicked after their candidate was forced to drop out, so they were running the parrot instead.

"An election shocker!" said Chad. "Captain Smek running against not one but *two* Earthlings. A human and a . . ." The newscaster checked his notes. "Bird."

"*Lower* taxes!" squawked the parrot. "Dynamic future!"

"That parrot is saying all the right things," observed Chad.

"Does the parrot have a name, Chad?" asked Bish.

Chad shuffled some papers. "At this time we believe it's Pop-Tart."

"Captain Smek," said the debate moderator. "Today in his broadcast the Squealer alleged that he *told* you about his connection to the Gorg retreat, and that you believed him. What do you have to say to that?"

Smek patted at the air with his hands. "Look: I think we are all now very confused about what is and what isn't. I can promise you that we will get to the bottom of the Squealer's claims, which I learned about at the same time as everybody else. But confusing times are no time for new leadership!" He leaned and looked slyly at Dan Landry. "Do not the humans themselves have a saying, 'You should not change horses in midstream'?"

This caused a ripple in the audience. Mostly a confused ripple—the Boov didn't know what a horse was, nor why you'd consider changing one in the first place. A poll taken after the debate would show that most assumed they were a kind of undergarment.

"New *leader*ship!" said Pop-Tart. "Crackers!"

Landry was too canny not to notice all the puzzled looks in the debate hall.

"On the contrary," he said with a smile. "Midstream is *exactly* where you want to change horses! The stream just washes the old horse away! No fuss!"

"Aha," the audience seemed to be saying at once. There was a lot of thoughtful nodding.

"Mr. Landry," said the moderator. "The Squealer's story casts doubt on your claim that *you* are the one responsible for the Gorg retreat—"

"Let me stop you there, if I may, to say that I never claimed to be a hero," said Landry, whose autobiography, *Just a Hero*, was projected on a screen behind him. "The Gorg retreat was the result of many good souls working together.

I'm told that you *Boov* have a saying, 'Many fingers make a hand.' I believe that too. I believe in all the Boovish people, such that I even brought my son here to learn from your great wisdom."

The camera cut to Emerson, in the audience. He looked bored.

"I think we all have a lot to teach each other," Landry concluded, "but we've learned everything we can from Captain Smek. He's the leader who either *knowingly* imprisoned an innocent Boov or allowed a guilty one to escape. New Boovworld deserves better, and that's why I want to be your president."

"A strong showing from Dan Landry tonight, Bish."

"Agreed. But environmentalists have to be wondering: What are his plans for our nation's streams? Will he fill them with horses?"

J.Lo came down the ramp from the bedroom. "I have arranged the shuttle!" he said. "It will arrive now in maybe thirty Earth minutes."

I was all butterflies. Anything might happen. The shuttle driver could recognize our faces and take us right to the police. Or we might get up to our parking space and find out our car had been impounded.

On the debate stage, someone new was joining Pop-Tart at his podium.

"Horses!" Pop-Tart was saying. "Brighter tomorrow!"

This new Boov put out an arm, and the parrot stepped onto it.

"We in the opposition party thank Pop-Tart for his service," said the Boov. "But the time has come for a candidate who is of the people and for the people. We nominate folk hero the Squealer for the position of HighBoov president of New Boovworld!"

"Ha!" I said, and choked on my milk shake.

"Whas?" said J.Lo, his English failing him. "No!"

The audience on TV was really reacting to this. Kind of a lot of cheering. Some boos, too, but not as many as you'd think. J.Lo dashed across the living room, dug the waveform device out of his bag, and snapped it over the television cables again.

"Um, hello?" he said, his big face all over the TV—which went "umhelloumhelloumelloumelloelloello" because we still had the sound on. J.Lo muted it. "Sorry. Sorry to interrupt a second time! Just wanted to say thank you, but I do not want to be president HighBoov. Thank you. Sorry."

He unclipped the waveform device, pressed mute again, and the TV snapped back to the debate. The audience was still cheering.

"That is just the reason why the Squealer is the people's choice!" said the guy with the parrot. "Who wants a leader who wants to be leader?" And I could see his point there. I've always sort of thought we ought to keep a close eye on anyone who wants power over others. But then the Boov added, "We want a leader who is just like us, but famous!" and he kind of lost me there. I want a leader who's a humble supergenius.

Anyway, the audience was eating it up. A couple of them had already managed to make signs. Smek and Landry blanched and winced at each other.

J.Lo had the waveform clip on again. "No, looksee," he told them. "I am no leader. I am just a simple maintenance Boov. A Boov who made a mistake and wanted to fix it. I—"

"Maa-aa-a-aa ma!" cried some of the koobish as they bolted across the living room, colliding and careening off me. It was like getting pelted by beach balls.

I looked to see what had scared them, and there was Funsize again in his bad-guy mask, every inch of his body just dripping guns.

One of the koobish kicked the TV box on its side, and now it wasn't J.Lo on the screen but the assassin, drawing a pair of pistols. He shouted, "DEATH TO—" in his robot voice before Bill gave him a face full of bubbles.

"FUH!" said Funsize. "WHAT?"

J.Lo unclipped the waveform device and began tossing koobish as he skirted around the room. He grabbed his bag and then my hand, and we dashed down the ramp to the street with Bill trailing behind.

Half the ramp got suddenly erased, and the rest collapsed

with J.Lo and me still on it. We tumbled onto our arms and faces, and I turned to see Funsize appear in the doorway above us. I was blocking his shot now, and I'd swear he was hesitating again. His mask made it impossible to tell if he was looking at me, but still—he was looking at me. The hovercart was out here, so I swung that around and hurled it at him as J.Lo got to his feet and started hopping and waving.

I thought he'd gone crazy until I looked up and saw the hot dog–shaped parking shuttle descending down into the alley. It extended a hoseleg for us.

"You firstnow," said J.Lo, trying to maneuver me under the hose. But I'm heavier.

"Don't be dumb!" I said, and I picked J.Lo up and threw him right up the hose. *FOOMP.* "He's not trying to kill *me*," I shouted after him, and turned to see Funsize pointing his guns, ready to prove me wrong. Then, *FOOMP*, the hose got me and Bill, too.

I popped up inside the shuttle, which was empty apart from J.Lo and the driver and was already rising slowly away from the alley.

"Can't you go faster?" I shouted, worried that Funsize would just shoot the whole thing full of holes. But as I watched out one of the windows, he disappeared back inside the bubble house.

"We made it!" said J.Lo. "Champions of the Galaxy! Thank you for picking us up, shuttle lady!"

The driver was actually saying something like "Anything for the Squealer" when Funsize appeared on the top of the bubble house and took a running leap at the shuttle.

Whap, he smacked into the side and held fast to the ledge of one of the porthole windows, the wind whipping him around. I watched him aim a pistol with his free hand and had only a moment to tackle J.Lo before the beam cut through the bus where his head had been. Funsize began climbing into the hole he'd made, so I rolled onto my side and kicked, knocking the gun out of his hand. But he had plenty more guns. Holsters held five more eraser pistols and a trombone rifle across his back and something that might have been a samurai sword. I tried to kick again, but Funsize grabbed my leg and used it to pull himself up.

Meanwhile, something was wrong with the shuttle. For starters, it was full of suds. Bill had clearly worked out that Funsize wanted to hurt J.Lo, so he was trying to make J.Lo impossible to find. But that hole Funsize had made with his pistol must have erased something important, because now the bus listed and turned, and the whole thing tipped upward and sent Funsize, J.Lo, and me sliding together through a bubbly blizzard toward the back seats. The driver was screaming. J.Lo caught hold of a handrail, but the assassin and I collapsed in a heap.

"GRATUITY!" he squawked as we wrestled. "You must not try to stop me!" I grabbed at him, trying to pin his arms, and ended up with one of his guns instead. He had so many guns it was hard *not* to grab one. Then the shuttle turned and tilted back and we separated—and in a moment we were both on our feet again, aiming pistols.

He had a gun pointed at my head. I had a gun pointed at his head. A couple of seconds passed.

You're probably waiting for me to tell you that I didn't shoot because I just couldn't take a life, right? I'm sorry to disappoint you. I was scared. I was scared, and full of fight-or-flight fizziness, and if I'd had a button I could have pressed in that moment to make Funsize disappear forever, I would have pressed it. I *did* have such a button. But so did he.

Honestly, whenever I'd see these kinds of standoffs in the movies, I'd always wonder why they didn't end right away. Wouldn't each gunman be trying to beat the other to the trigger? But it turns out you just stand there, watching the other guy's finger. If it twitches, you die. But he'll die too. You'll have just enough time to make sure of that. You don't want to die, and he doesn't want to die, so you both end up standing there. Watching fingers.

Meanwhile, your brain's busy firing all over the place. You think of your mom, and J.Lo, but you also remember your third-grade dance recital for some reason—the one where you played Potassium and tripped on your own banana peel. And you remember something important, suddenly, about a Boov you met in a pagoda made of garbage.

"You called me Gratuity," I told the assassin, my hands trembling. "Twice now you've called me that. I told *Funsize* that my name was Grace." I squinted at him. "Who *are* you?"

The shuttle was nodding forward, slowly somersaulting. The driver had stopped screaming, which was nice, but it was only because she'd fainted, which was less so. J.Lo loosed his grip and dropped to the front of the bus, where he shoved the driver out of her seat and tried to grapple with the controls.

The shuttle was still tipping, and leaking bubbles, and the assassin and I were still pointing guns at each other. I could reach a handrail from where I was, but in a second the assassin was going to lose his traction and fall into me. I don't think either one of us knew what was going to happen after that.

"How you doing back there, J.Lo?" I called.

J.Lo took a while to answer. "Fine," he said finally.

"J.Lo?"

"Yes. Out of curiosity, how many buildings are too many buildings to crash into?"

"THIS IS NOT OVERNOW," said the assassin, and he raised his gun and made a hole in the roof of the bus, and the side. Then he inflated his suit, and out he jumped.

"Jeez," I whispered. I let go of the rail and joined J.Lo in the cab. He couldn't get the controls to do anything he wanted. Directly ahead was a bell-jar tower, coming up fast as the shuttle swiveled and spun.

"The assassin—he left?" asked J.Lo.

"He left," I panted.

"Why did he leave?"

"He probably thought we were doing a pretty good job of assassinating ourselves," I answered, nodding at the looming tower. "Anybody live in that?"

"No! Is a supercomputer, filledto with computer gas!"

I aimed my gun and made a hole through the front window of the shuttle, and then another in the side of the tower. Pressurized gas shooshed out, and I held my breath, trying to inhale as few microprocessors as possible. I couldn't see anything, but I kept firing, and what was left of the bus tumbled into the tower, and downward through the tower, and out another hole I made in the opposite side. The gas cleared, and a big telecloner came up fast.

"AAH!" said J.Lo, straining against the steering column, his knuckles hot pink.

I erased the telecloner, too. I was starting to enjoy myself a little. But now a football field was closing in.

Well, not a football field, obviously, but that was my first impression. A ring of stadium seats surrounding a big expanse of powder-blue grass with two end zones. No yard markings, but three chalk circles topped with bubbles. Boov on the field, playing stickyfish. Boov in the stands. So many people.

"J.Lo!"

"I know!"

If we kept diving in the same direction, we were going to hit the stands. J.Lo pulled the bus into a tight spin, and we did doughnuts as the whole craft slowly sank toward the grass. Uniformed stickyfish players ran to avoid us, and now the bus was only a few meters above the ground.

"Can you straighten us out?" I yelled. He did his best. Then I grabbed his wrist and ran for the rear of the shuttle, shooting all the way—shooting left and right and up and down and blasting as many holes in the bus's walls as I could. We jumped and rolled out onto the field as mere bits and pieces of what was once a functioning parking shuttle skidded and came apart behind us.

We lay there for a minute, scraped and bruised, our chests rising and falling. Bill circled once and perched on my face.

The stickyfish game was still in play. Apparently the rules don't let you call a time-out for something as trifling as a bus crash.

Without stirring, J.Lo asked, "How dead are you?"

"Only a little bit dead," I told him.

"I am less dead than I had anticipated."

I got up on my elbows. There was a Boov in pink standing inside the closest bubble and looking for a teammate to pass the fish to. Other Boov in yellow guarded the bubble but apparently weren't allowed inside. But while the pink guy with the fish was in there, a Boov in yellow entered a different bubble and shouted "Safetybubbletrouble!" and play paused as possession of the fish changed sides. The referees decided this was a good time to break and clean pieces of parking shuttle off the field.

Stickyfish players stood and stared at us, and whispered to one another. One of the referees came up and gave J.Lo and me yellow flags. The crowd was cheering, a fog of sound.

Then that now-familiar electronic voice cut suddenly through the fog.

"J.LO! I AM COMING FOR YOU, WORLD KILLER!"

I groaned. "Good of him to warn us, I guess," I said, wobbling to my feet. Bill zipped about, looking at all the people. I peered around us and saw field, and players and stands, and some dull orange cylinders in the breezeways where the stands exited into the streets.

"C'mon," I said, yanking J.Lo along toward one of the breezeways. The Boov in the seats seemed pretty psyched to be seeing the Squealer. A few booed.

"Ignore them," I said, and pulled J.Lo over to the nearest orange cylinder. This garbage can was bigger than the ones in the palace—more of a Dumpster than a wastebasket.

"We can no hide in there," said J.Lo. "We will get sucked downward to the chompers."

"Trust me," I said, and hopped inside the garbage tunnel, pulling him down after me.

SIXTEEN

This tunnel was so wide that it was hard not to get going *too* fast. I stretched out my legs and tried to put the brakes on with the rubber soles of my shoes. But then my feet actually got hot and I had to let us go into free fall again until they cooled down, so that was a pain. Plus all the screaming.

"AAAAAAAAAAAAAAAAAAAAAAAAAAAAAAAAAAAAAAAA WE ARE GOING TO DIE NOW," J.Lo said unhelpfully.

And I guess I could see how he'd think that when our tunnel sucked us to the right and then straightened out again and we could hear the crisp metal chomp of the chompers getting louder. I jammed my feet against the sides again, but we barely slowed. Bill flew on ahead and sprayed us with bubbles as we rounded another bend. Through all that carbonation I could just barely see the chomper's sharp trap opening and closing in front of us.

But I still had one of the assassin's guns, right? So I aimed to make a big cavity in those teeth.

"Bill!" I shouted. "Out of the way!" And when he moved, I fired. But nothing happened. I fired again.

"Why isn't this working?!" I screamed.

"You have been to firing it a lot!" said J.Lo. "May be out of charge!"

I pulled the trigger again and again, then banged the whole gun a few times against the tunnel walls, and the chompers were about to take off my legs when I fired one final time and we dropped twenty feet into a pile of gray slop.

I looked up.

"Got 'em," I said, jerking my chin above us at the big hole I'd made and the scraps of teeth that were left, jawing uselessly at nothing. "Good plan, amirite?"

"Meh," said J.Lo.

"Any landing you can walk away from," I began.

"Cannot walk. Stuck in slop."

* * *

Turned out we could walk, but barely.

"I want ONE HUNDRED showers," said J.Lo.

I've never really believed in hell, pardon my language. God has to have a better plan than an all-or-nothing reality game show. But if you wanted to imagine hell, you could do worse than trudging knee-deep through a hot subterranean swamp of liquid garbage while a thousand rusty metal mouths bite and bite endlessly above you.

"How far do you suppose we were from the palace when we crashed?" I asked.

"Mmmmaybies three miles."

"And how far do you think we have left?"

"Also three miles."

It was a long time before we saw Funsize's death-ray pagoda in the distance. Bill scouted ahead to have a look at it.

"There," I said. "That's where he lives. See? He has solid garbage around his place 'cause the nearest chomper doesn't work."

"This is my life now," said J.Lo. "I am all jazzed at the promise of solid garbage."

"Okay," I panted. "You'd better let me approach first, J.Lo. You're not exactly his favorite person—"

But just then Bill returned and spelled something complicated in the air above us.

"What did that say?" I asked.

"Hm. It said that this Funsize is no at home."

Then the garbage rumbled, and shifted, and the periscope of Funsize's little submarine sprouted up between us.

Through the periscope his happy, muffled voice said, "It is you!"

We stepped back as the whole contraption surfaced and the bubble retracted.

"Yeah, hi, Funsize," I said, "it's me—"

But the little Boov drew up to J.Lo with anxious fingers. "The *Squealer,*" he whispered. "Right here in my home!"

"Yes hello," said J.Lo, waving.

Funsize was actually a bit shorter than J.Lo, now that I saw them together. I couldn't believe I'd once thought this weird little person was the assassin. But *still—*

"Uh," I began, uncertain. "Now I know you're upset with J.Lo, Funsize, but I think—"

"Upset by the *Squealer*? Well, yes—once," he admitted, taking J.Lo's hands. "But I heard you on the news. You were just a simple maintenance Boov. A Boov who made a mistake, and wanted to *fix* it. It is just like my story! You are me!"

"Aha," said J.Lo. "Okaythen."

"And soon you will be president HighBoov! It is very exciting. Come," he said, leading J.Lo by the wrist. "Come to the pa-GOH-da."

It was easier going here, where the garbage wasn't slop. Funsize's submarine was only a one-person vehicle, but he piloted it alongside us with the top open.

"Soooo, Funsize," I said, trying to choose my words delicately. "This mistake *you* made—the one that got you sent here in the first place—do I want to know what it was?"

Funsize got a far-off look. "I loved . . . *too much,*" he sighed.

So the answer was no, I didn't want to know what it was.

J.Lo craned back to look at Funsize's home.

"Hm," he said. "Death ray."

Funsize clasped his hands and stepped forward. He was as big-eyed as a puppy. "Do you like it?"

"An interesting design," J.Lo said, nodding. "But how could you power such a thing?"

Funsize waggled his hands. "I used one of the digger robots and tapped into the fiery core at the *center of the moon!*"

"Whoa," said J.Lo, impressed. "Hm. Now that is an interesting idea."

"Funsize," I said, "my name isn't Grace. It's Gratuity. But you can call me Tip. I know that's stupidly confusing and I'm sorry about that. Also, I lost your hoverbutt."

"It is okay. I have two others."

Funsize gave J.Lo a tour of his house. I was only interested in getting clean, so he showed me how his submarine doubled as a sort of dishwasher for people. After I was dry, I reentered the pagoda.

J.Lo was saying, "But I do not want to be president HighBoov. I do not want the power."

"And that is just why everybody loves you!" said Funsize, bouncing in his chair. "Plus they saw on the NewsFeed the way Captain Smek tried to have you assassinated. To keep you from talking the truth!"

"Oh, man," I said, coming in. "That guy was working for Smek?"

Funsize shrugged. "It is what everyBoov thinks."

"Can they elect you anyway?" I asked J.Lo. "Even if you don't want it?"

"I do not know. But I will not let them find me. I am going to stay here and work on my time machine."

I winced. But Funsize nearly fell off his chair, he was so happy.

"You will live with me!" he squealed. "We can make garbage farts to sleep in!"

I touched my translator. "That should have been 'forts,' right?"

"Sadly, no," said J.Lo.

"Sooo," I said, "I thought the time machine idea was dead. Needed too much energy."

"Ahyes! We have been talking, Funsize and I. The moon's core can fuel my time machine, so long as you do not mind me stealing power from your death ray, Funsize."

The garbage Boov waved a hand. "Oh, I was probably going to dismantle it," he said. "A death ray in the home is more likely to be used against a loved one than on your enemies anyway. Statistically."

I took a breath. "This plan . . . doesn't sound like it would put us any closer to getting home," I said.

I was feeling like a rubber band. I was feeling like a

rubber band stretched all the way from Earth to this pagoda, and every time I thought it was time to snap back home, it got pulled just a little farther away. And I was going to break, I swear I was.

"Actualies," said J.Lo, "if the trip is successful, it will be liketo you never left!"

I wasn't ready to deal with this, so I said, "Hey, Funsize, do you have any idea if Dan Landry is still staying in the palace?"

"It is what they say on the NewsFeed, yes."

"Okay, well, I totally wouldn't blame you if you said no, but: Can I borrow another hoverbutt?"

"Heh," said J.Lo. "Hoverbutt."

SEVENTEEN

Funsize didn't know where exactly Dan Landry's quarters would be. But the gossip feeds were buzzing with the rumor that Landry and Smek were going to run together to counter the threat of a J.Lo presidency, so he suggested I might find both of them in the Oval Office.

It was a good instinct. As Bill and I neared the lid of the garbage can in Smek's office, I could already hear their stupid voices.

"One thing I cannot budge on is my role as top commander," Smek was saying. "We cannot share this."

Landry harrumphed. "Well, I can't see how it's a co-presidency if one of us is claiming some of the power all for himself."

"But can you imagine the Boovish armies following a human into battle, now? It is madness."

"Hmm. I *guess* I wouldn't mind you being commander in chief if I get to appoint all the judges."

"Hoo! You are wanting to appoint judges? You're welcome to *that* basket of headaches."

"Say," said Landry, "will there be much vetoing? I think I'd really like to veto something."

Smek let out a happy sigh. "Vetoes are the *best.*"

I figured I'd heard enough of that, so we ducked back down the tunnel and up the next closest garbage can, which I figured would be in the waiting room next to the secretary's desk.

The secretary was already gone for the day, but the waiting room wasn't entirely empty. Emerson sat in one of those sticky chairs, reading the *Ladies' Home Journal.* And not reading it too closely, I guess, because he noticed me right away.

He squinted. "Hello?" he said. "Is there . . . are you in the garbage can?"

I pushed up the lid and climbed out, lugging the hoverbutt behind me. "Hey," I said. "You're Emerson, right?" I watched the door to Smek's office as I joined him by the chairs and potted plants.

"You're the girl from the TV."

"Gratuity. My friends call me Tip."

"You and that Boov are the real ones who saved the Earth, instead of my dad."

"Uh, yeah, I guess. Sorry."

Emerson sank deeper into his chair and shrugged, like he hadn't figured out how he felt about it yet. "Is that a bee?"

"His name is Bill," I said.

The door behind me opened and Landry entered reception, saying, "Okay, talk soon," over his shoulder. The door closed behind him, and he stopped cold when he saw me. I beamed him a smile, but my smile was, like, deflected by powerful force fields and ended up under a chair somewhere.

"Gratuity Tucci," he said, and straightened his shirt cuffs. "It's been a while. How's your mother?"

"Good," I said. "Actually . . . probably angry. Probably so angry she's setting things on fire with her mind. Which is why I was hoping to talk to y—"

"Your little friend is making this quite the exciting race!" said Landry. He was already on the move, so Emerson fell in behind him, and Bill and I fell in behind Emerson. "What were you and Lucy calling him in Arizona? JayJay? Back when he was your brother?"

We were walking across that open skywalk to the elevator. I felt very exposed. Now that J.Lo had explained everything on live TV, I wasn't sure if we were in the clear.

"He's . . . still my brother," I said. "And he goes by J.Lo."

"J.Lo?" Emerson repeated.

Landry smirked. "Well, *J.Lo* is causing a lot of trouble for New Boovworld. Disrupting the electoral process. It's a two-party system. He should drop out."

"What?" I almost fell off the walkway. "He doesn't even *want* to be president! He's just telling the truth!"

"Is he? One Boov doesn't get to just decide what is true and not true, Gratuity. We have polls for that. I mean, why should we trust anything he says? He's been *in jail*. He has an *arrest record*. Where did he even come from, anyway?" Landry paused, thinking. "You know, I don't think either Smek or J.Lo was born in this solar system." He bit his lip. "Wonder if I could get any traction out of that."

I got between them and the elevator. "Look, I'm sorry. I didn't come here to fight. I . . . actually need a favor."

"Aha. And this is you buttering me up, is it?"

"I'm kind of having trouble getting home. I was wondering if I could get a ride when you guys go back to Earth."

Landry squared his shoulders. "Well, until the voters have their say, I can't tell you for certain that we *are* going back to Earth."

You could see this catch Emerson off guard.

"But . . ." I said. "C'mon, though. There's no way you're ever winning that election."

"He might!" Emerson said, red-faced. "He deserves to, because . . ." The boy trailed off and looked up at his dad. "I'm sorry. I couldn't come up with anything."

Landry ignored his son. Ignored him with an ease that only comes from lots of practice. I missed Mom.

"Make you a deal, Gratuity. I'll send you back. I'll send you back to Mother tomorrow! *If* you go on TV and say that J.Lo's whole story of teleporting and cat cloning is a lie."

I kind of recoiled. But he rounded his palms around my shoulders, patted my back with his fingers.

"This is a serious offer, Gratuity. There's no one coming from home to get you, no regular New Boovworld–to–Earth flights waiting to take you back, but I can make it happen. Just go on TV, say that it was your pal Dan Landry who turned back the Gorg. You'll do it, if you really believe in truth."

I frowned. "That . . . makes no sense."

"Sure it does—if the truth's as strong as you say, then a little bending can't hurt it." He straightened. "You think about it. We're in room 4-440 when you're ready to talk. Come on, Emerson."

Emerson followed him into the elevator, and they both turned—Landry gazing stoically over my head at a Dan Landry Tomorrow or whatever, Emerson squinting like he was trying to decide whether he was going to call me Tip or not. Then the doors closed and we were alone on the catwalk.

"Come on, Bill," I said, and I turned to go back down to the garbage pile, which was suddenly not the grossest place I'd been today.

EIGHTEEN

I went back into the pagoda through the front door, but nobody was around. Funsize had mentioned a basement, so I poked around until I found the door. It was set flush into the central pillar, covered by a girlie poster.

I looked at Bill. "You gonna be offended if I want to go talk to J.Lo alone?" I asked.

Bill was still for a moment before answering.

YES.

"Come on," I said. "It's nothing against you. It's just that I've known J.Lo a long time, and what I'm about to ask him . . . it's delicate. I think it'll be better to ask him in private."

BATHROOM, said Bill, because that was one of the only words I could read.

"Right. Private like a bathroom."

Another pause.

NO, said Bill, bigger than usual, and he turned to fart some confetti at me before buzzing away.

I watched him go. "Yeah, that seems about right," I sighed, and opened the door.

Inside the hollow pillar was a winding ramp, and I followed it around and around and downward and now I was dizzy and had to spend a minute propping myself up against the wall. Then around and around and ever downward until I bottomed out and passed through a second door into a vast cavern beneath the trash.

The pillar was connected to massive cables that snaked like anacondas across a floor of metal grating to an open pit, where J.Lo and Funsize were working.

It was super hot down here, and stale. A dusky red glow rippled up from the pit. I walked over the metal floor, and J.Lo raised his head.

"You are back! Comesee. We are making top-quality progress."

J.Lo had the makings of a dense cube of tubes and shapes with two straps so he could wear it like a backpack. One tube in particular spooled out to a medium-sized gray thing that J.Lo was poking with tiny pink things.

"Funsize was just telling me about the ladyBoov he used to work with—"

"Yeah, hey—Funsize?" I said. "Can I have a minute alone to talk to J.Lo about something? Sorry."

"Oh!" said Funsize. "Yes."

"Sorry."

"No, it is good. I should be checking on my muffins anyways."

He got up and walked to the pillar. I heard the door open and close behind me.

"J.Lo," I said.

I had a serious tone, and he stopped his tinkering to look at me.

I said, "Please don't do this."

He lowered his hands. "Do not do whatnow?"

"Don't make a time machine. Don't go back and cancel your signal to the Gorg. It . . ." I puffed a fake little laugh through my nose. "It won't even work. Time travel never works."

"It does not do?"

"No, I mean, look at all the stories in books and movies and whatever. You'll just end up being the cause of whatever you've gone back to prevent."

"Ahyes. I know these stories. I think that is a lazy author problem, not a time travel problem." He smiled. After a moment he seemed to think we'd settled it, and he went back to poking at the gray thing with the pink thing.

"Then . . . don't do it because I'm *asking* you not to do it," I said. "Don't do it for me."

"For . . . you?" I could see he didn't understand. "You are saying you . . . wish for to have the Gorg did come?"

I puzzled through that hall of mirrors and decided yes, that was probably what I was saying. J.Lo was speaking English, as he always did when it was just the two of us, but the grammar of time travel was giving him more trouble than usual.

"Yeah. I mean, why mess with it? Everything turned out okay."

"Ha! This is one of those humansjokes I do not get? Everything has *not* done turned out okay."

"Sure it has!" I said, faking enthusiasm. "Sure! The Gorg retreated! Now your people will know how to fight them if they ever come back! And the Boov see now that you're the hero you really are. I mean, *I* don't want the humans to know about *my* part in the whole deal, but . . ."

J.Lo seemed to be turning it over in his mind. "No," he said finally. "It willto have done been better after I will had cancel the signal, I am thinking. You are worried that we will never had became friends? I think we will have did. Listen, I have a plan—"

"J.Lo!" I stopped him. I was hacking at the air with my hands, angry with him for making me say it. "J.Lo. How will we get rid of the Boov?"

Quiet. Just the hum of the diggers.

"Ahyes," J.Lo said. "The Boov. I can to make it so that the

Gorg did never have come, but Gratuity wants to know how we get rid of the Boov."

He called me Gratuity. Which he only ever does when he's mad.

"They . . . never would have given Earth back if the Gorg hadn't come," I said. "I know how to get rid of Gorg. I never *did* figure out the Boov."

"Gratuity," he said. "A thousand brave Boov died fighting the Gorg. A thousand people."

And then I saw them: a thousand Boov crowding his shoulders, weighing him down. He'd been carrying them around with him for a year and a half—why hadn't I seen them before?

"Alls of them. Deadnow. Because of a mistake *I* made. What about them?"

I searched my hands for the answer, stupidly. Like on my palms were everybody's lifelines, like I could read them and see where they'd lead if we acted, see where they'd end if we did nothing.

"I don't know," I admitted with a weak shrug. "I don't know about them. But what about seven *billion* humans? Moved out of their homes? Treated like dumb animals?"

J.Lo got up, marched around gathering up junk in his arms. "I cannot have this conversation. I will go back, I will have done stopped the signal. Because it will then seemlike the antenna malfunctioned, theretofore past J.Lo will not to leave the antenna farm too quickly, and he/me will still then have met Gratuity. Gratuity will still have teached to me the true meaning of humanskind. So I will convince then the Boov to leave. *That* is how we get rid of the Boov."

"But why would the Boov listen to y—"

"Have you not noticed now? I am very famous and beloved!"

"But only because—"

He dropped all his stuff and waved his little hands. "I will get famous and beloved for some *others* thing! I will discover a hilarious song! Or the cure for bigface!"

"Okay, you know what?" I said, stiff as a pin. "Forget it. Go monkey around with the past. And when you get around to the part where we're supposed to meet and make friends? Don't bother!"

I thundered out, my face a hot mess. J.Lo shouted something after me, but my mole didn't translate it. Or couldn't.

Must've been pretty bad.

NINETEEN

"Where you goin', kid?" the Chief asked me.

"You know where I'm going," I muttered as I crossed rooms to elevators and walked up ramps to Level 4. Palace workers paused to look at me, but I didn't look back. Eyes forward, walking briskly but not running, I looked like I was supposed to be there. Like I had urgent business. Don't bother the human with stupid questions; she obviously has somewhere to be. "You disappointed in me too?" I asked the Chief. "You going to abandon me like everybody else?"

Ahead of me was a skywalk. At the end of that was Dan Landry's door.

The Chief eyed me. "What in God's name are you talking about, Stupidlegs?"

"J.Lo's abandoning me. Bill . . . abandoned me.

You died. My dad was *never* around, and Mom . . ."

I trailed off, without a clue how to finish that sentence. The Chief blew a raspberry.

the Chief

"You know, I'll wager the Spook thinks *you* abandoned *him*. Bill just got his feelings hurt, but cut him some slack—he's new at feelings. *I* loved you like a granddaughter, and your pa didn't know he had a kid and still doesn't. And please explain about your ma—"

"All right, I know—"

"—'cause to the casual observer it looks more like you're the one who flew eight hundred million miles away from her."

"All *right!*"

I frowned. But there wasn't any time to think about it. The Chief was gone and I was looking at the door to room 4-440. My own ravaged face was reflected back in its mirror finish.

When it opened, I couldn't look Dan Landry in the eye. Mostly I just didn't want him to know I'd been crying.

"Gratuity Tucci, as I live and breathe," he said. "Made up your mind so fast?"

I sniffed, and stared at his shoes. They were nice shoes.

"I just want to go home," I said quietly.

He stood aside and let me in.

It was a big suite, with plush furniture and a giant screen and end tables everywhere. Emerson was reading a comic book atop a big blue pouf. He looked surprised to see me.

"I told Captain Smek about our arrangement," said Landry. He put his hand on the small of my back and steered me across the room. "He furnished me with a device that will let you interrupt all the video feeds the same way your little friend did. We think it's important that it look the same, you understand me?"

"And then I go back home?" I asked. "Just like that?"

"Just like that. I had the Boov find your car. They'll tow it all the way back to Earth with you in it. I told you I'm a man who can make things happen, Gratuity. Now: Do you know what you're going to say?"

I nodded.

"Don't just nod; tell me."

I sighed. "It's . . . I'm not going to go on and on saying how great you are or anything. It's gonna be short."

Landry nodded and twirled his hand. He seemed to be in a hurry.

"Well," I said, "I'm gonna say that I'm the human, Gratuity Tucci, and that J.Lo's my friend—"

"Call him the Squealer, actually."

"That . . . the Squealer's my friend, but that he lied about all that stuff he said. The whole story. That I went along with it because . . . he's my friend. But I know and everyone on Earth knows that Dan Landry defeated the Gorg."

"Fine. Smek also wants some language added about how Dan Landry was able to beat the Gorg only because Captain Smek had loosened them up first. Like they're a pickle jar. I told him I'd write it down for you, but . . ." He was putting on his suit jacket and watch and looking constantly at the door. "You seem articulate enough. Just wing the Smek stuff. Or don't, I really don't care."

"You're leaving?" asked Emerson. "Now?"

"Pressing business," Landry told him. "Remember what we talked about."

Emerson looked miserable. "Yeah, I know," he said.

"Gratuity? Clip the thing when you're ready to talk. Unclip it when you're done. You're doing the right thing. We're all doing the right thing. Onward and upward. No regrets," he finished as the suite door opened and closed and he was gone.

When that much chatter is suddenly gone, it leaves kind of a dizzy vacuum in its place. I swooned and looked at my hands.

"For a while I thought you wouldn't come up here," Emerson told me after a moment, with a stony expression that said he had me *all* figured out now.

"Whatever," I muttered, and turned to the TV. Another cooking show on mute. Some improbable-looking vegetable sizzled silently on a grill. A lone Boov worked over a metal grate lit by a dusky red glow. I eyed Smek's waveform clip.

Just do it quick, I thought, like ripping off a Band-Aid— and I took up the waveform device and snapped it in place.

Now I was on the TV. My face, parade-balloon big.

I thought of all the Boov all over New Boovworld, pausing in their lives, wondering what I was going to say. There was a slight delay between me and this giant girl on the screen. I'd move slightly; she'd move slightly a fraction of a second later. Like the giant girl wasn't me, but just a show I was watching.

And I thought, That's how I'm going to get through this.

I thought, It's not me.

The giant girl looked tired. She needed a change of clothes.

I took a breath, the girl took a breath, and said, "Hi."

I could feel my heart. I imagined all of New Boovworld saying hi back.

"I'm the human, Gratuity Tucci. J.Lo . . . the *Squealer* is my friend. And I have something really important to tell you about Dan Landry."

I found myself wishing I could comfort the giant girl on the screen—look at those puffy eyes, that hair. If she were *my* friend, I realized, I'd probably tell her to call her mother.

(She wasn't, though. She was about to badmouth J.Lo.)

But then if her mother was anything like my mother, she'd be better off solving her *own* problems. Mom had been so not *there* when I was growing up that when she got sucked right out of my life by a spaceship, it was like the punch line to a joke that hadn't been funny for years, you know?

The sick feeling in my stomach told me that I was full of it. Even the girl on the screen was shaking her head.

We both took a breath.

"Don't be like me," I told her. "Don't be afraid to trust people; don't be afraid to love."

Of course, by telling *her* this, I was really telling it to a million Boov. That must have been confusing.

"Sorry. So. I have something important to tell you about Dan Landry. Did I say that already?"

Look at that, now—the girl just got this gleam in her eye. She looked good. She looked like someone the Chief would have liked. I couldn't believe what she was going to say next.

"Dan Landry is a poomp," she said. I said.

"A real kacknacker," I added. "Pardon my language."

She had a nice smile, this girl.

"I just thought you should know."

TWENTY

I unclipped the waveform dealie and turned to leave.

Emerson was standing between me and the door.

"My dad asked me to keep you here," he said. "To stop you."

I snorted. "Stop me?"

Emerson swallowed. "I don't think he's noticed that I'm shorter than all the girls in my class."

I took a step toward Emerson. He took a step back.

"So what's *your* dad like?" he asked.

The question surprised me, and I halted.

"I . . . don't know," I said.

"I was six when I lost my first tooth," Emerson said. "It was in the summer, so my dad had me."

I couldn't stop looking at the door. Probably made me

seem rude. "Okay," I said. I couldn't imagine where he was going with this.

"So I told my dad, and he said to put the tooth under my pillow that night. My best friend had already lost two teeth, so I knew about this. I knew what was coming." He shifted. "I went to bed with the tooth under my pillow, and the next morning I found ten dollars under there instead."

I raised my eyebrows at this. In my house the going rate was a quarter.

"So I ran out to the kitchen with my ten bucks," said Emerson. "And I asked who put it under my pillow. And Dad said, 'I did!'"

I frowned. "What, no Tooth Fairy?"

"That's what *I* said. I asked him, 'What about the Tooth Fairy?' and Dad said, '*I'm* the Tooth Fairy! Me.' Then he went back to reading his paper."

"Yeesh," I said. "That's kind of rough."

"It's always . . . it is always always *always* about him." He sighed. "When do most kids stop believing in the Tooth Fairy? Like, at what age?"

"Dunno," I said. "Seven or eight?"

Emerson nodded, and looked backward at the spot where he'd last seen his father. "Yeah. Yeah, that's when I mostly stopped too."

We stared at each other in silence for a minute.

Finally he said, "Let me get the door for you."

And he did, and that was nice, but the gesture was sort of ruined by the six armed Boov who were standing on the skywalk outside.

I was used to this sort of thing, but it took Emerson a minute to figure it out.

"Wh . . ." he said. "What are you all doing here?"

The Boov in the front answered as the others leveled their weapons.

"We have been ordered to prevent the humansgirl from leaving your chambers."

"Oh . . . there . . . there must be some misunderstanding. My dad asked *me* to keep her here. He probably forgot to tell Captain Smek."

The Boov exchanged looks.

"It was from your father that we received our orders," said the Boov in front. "Captain Smek has made him a sergeant."

"I heard lieutenant," said another Boov.

"Rear admiral," I suggested.

Emerson was red in the face. "It was *my* job! My dad left *me* to keep her here!"

The Boov looked back flatly. "But you failed."

"But my dad didn't *know* I was gonna fail!"

One of the other Boov gave him a strained smile. "Yyyyeah, he did, though."

Emerson was shaking a little, clenching his fists. I was afraid he might do something stupid.

The Boov in the lead said, "Humansgirl, step back into Dan Landry's quarters and await further instructions."

I crossed my arms.

"No," I said.

The Boov blinked.

"No whatnow?"

"No, I won't step back into Dan Landry's quarters," I said.

He glanced back at his teammates, then leaned forward and addressed me.

"But you *have* to step back into Dan Landry's—"

"But I don't *want* to do it," I said. "I don't want to. I'm going to walk back across this skywalk and go downstairs and help my friend, 'cause he's my friend."

The Boov chewed his lip. "This has never happened before," he said. "Would you excuse us a moment?"

"Sure."

Emerson and I stood there as the Boov huddled up.

"What are we to do?" asked one.

"Shoot her," said another.

"We are not allowed to shoot her. Captain Smek said so." They looked down at their weapons.

"I do not know why I am even carrying this thing."

The guards huddled closer, and I couldn't make out what they were saying anymore. One of them leaned back and mimed a plan with his hands to the others, something to do with rope and a lot of waving and maybe a bird. Finally the knot of them opened to face me.

"Thank you for your patience," said the leader. "We have come to a decision; we are going to—"

But that was when they were bombarded with bubbles and fell off the skywalk.

"Bill!" I cheered. "You came back!"

The little bluzzer hovered over the now-empty skywalk. *YES.*

Emerson was looking over the edge at the falling Boov. "They inflated their suits," he said. "They're all bouncing around down there."

"Are you still mad at me, Bill?" I asked.

YES.

"Why?"

Bill spilled forth two dozen bubbles of different shapes and sizes. I couldn't follow it.

"You know I can't read that, Bill."

Emerson stepped forward. "It says, 'I am . . . mad about the bluzzer on your back.' Oh, right—you have a bluzzer on your back; did you know that?"

"What?" I craned my neck to look.

Then I saw it in my reflection in the mirrored door: a little silver bee, smaller than Bill. It was on my shoulder blade. *Right* where Dan Landry had patted me a few hours ago.

"Sonofa—" I whispered. I brushed at the bluzzer, and it took off. It was probably one of those homing beacons, and it had been on my back for *hours*. I'd led Smek and Landry right to J.Lo.

"We have to get underground," I said. "I think J.Lo's in trouble."

TWENTY-ONE

Bill and I raced across the catwalk, through a bubble room, past Boov and more Boov, down a slide, and to the elevator, and now I noticed that Emerson was following. He got into the elevator with us and took up his elevator pose, standing stock-still and facing front.

"Um," I said. "Are you going on this rescue with us?"

Emerson looked at me and flushed. "Yeah! I mean, if that's okay."

YES.

I said, "Well. You know if we're going to be rescuing my friend from anyone, it'll be your dad. Smek too, maybe, but—your dad."

Emerson faced forward again. The elevator slowed. "I know. I mean, if you don't trust me, I can take this elevator back up to our room . . ."

That stung, like my own thoughts were coming back to me in the form of this weird little blond kid. The elevator door shooshed open, and Bill and I exited. Emerson stayed in there, watching us.

I held the door. "Trusting people more is this new thing I'm gonna try from now on," I said. "Don't make me regret it, okay?"

Emerson grinned and practically pranced out of the elevator, then tried to look cool, then grinned again. "Where now?"

"Garbage pit," I said.

After I slid down through tubes and past the wrecked chomper and landed in the trash next to Emerson, I saw his pained face looking back at me.

"When you said 'garbage pit,' I thought it was a figure of speech," he said.

"It wasn't."

"Like when people say they're 'in the belly of the whale' but they're not really in the belly of a whale."

"Nope, literal garbage pit."

We slogged and waded toward the pagoda.

"Bill!" I sort of shout-whispered. "Why didn't you tell me there was another bluzzer on my back?"

Bill spelled out all kinds of complicated stuff. Emerson squinted at it.

"Um . . ." he said. "Well, I've only been studying Boovish for like a year, but it's like he thought you knew it was there. I don't think he understands how a human could have something like that on them and not know it. He thought you'd made a new bee friend and he got jealous? Or something?"

I sighed. "Oh, Bill. I didn't know, I swear. You're the only bee for me."

YES.

We crept up to the pagoda, the three of us, and peeked inside. Nothing. But the door to the basement was open, and *I* hadn't left it that way.

"Follow me," I whispered.

I stepped lightly into Funsize's home and cast about for some kind of weapon. The gun I'd had earlier was out of juice, and besides, I didn't want to erase anyone. Instead I found a couple of heavy tools, like a cross between a pipe wrench and those little wooden things you use to serve honey. One of them was larger than the other, so I gave Emerson the small one. Then we started down the ramp to the basement.

Turning and turning we descended, until I threw out an arm and stopped us both about halfway down. I'd heard something. Voices. I crept closer, carefully.

"What are they saying?" whispered Dan Landry, below. "Was that the Squealer or the one with the mask and gun?"

Gun? I gasped. The assassin?

"I do not know and also I do not care," said Captain Smek. "Just keep the camera on them. Not on me, on them!"

"Sorry," said Landry.

There was another voice, a distant voice. It sounded like J.Lo, sort of.

"I invented a time machine too, you see," this voice was saying. "And when I fired it up, there was then a rumble, and terrible heat, and I saw the planet's core go CRITICAL-NOVA! And start to *EXPLORE!*"

"Did he say 'time machine'?" whispered Landry over the sounds of more distant conversation.

"Quiet and keep videoing," said Smek. "And do *not* point the camera at me when I put the waveform device on the stabilizers!"

"But this is definitely safe," Landry said. "Of course."

"Of course. It will cause momentary tremors and then I will take it off. And our video will show what looks like the Squealer trying to destroy New Boovworld."

I turned, and waved for Emerson and Bill to head back up the ramp. When we were farther up I explained what I wanted to do, and Bill flew back down.

Emerson and I waited on either side of the basement door with our weird tools. He was breathing hard. I guess I was too.

"When they appear . . ." I said. "When they appear, do you want to hit Smek, or your dad? I'd understand if you'd rather hit Sm—"

"I want to hit my dad," said Emerson.

224

TWENTY-TWO

The Boovish military police held us all—J.Lo and Dark J.Lo and me and Emerson and Smek and Landry and even Bill—in the Oval Office until they figured out the whole story. But luckily Smek and Landry had been videoing the whole thing, so there was never really any doubt.

"It was a joke!" Smek was saying. "A funny joke!" They had him confined to a little office chair in the middle of the room, and anytime he looked like he might be trying to stand and make speeches, a trio of grim-looking guards stared at him until he sat down again. "Seriously, a joke," he added, more quietly. "You should all see your faces!"

Their faces looked like this:

Another guard was way up near the skylight, messing around with Smek's throne, opening and closing the turret. I guess he didn't realize the hologram was projecting his head all giant-size over the floor below or he wouldn't have been picking his teeth like that.

Dan Landry sat miserably in a different chair, surrounded by different guards, smack in the center of that tooth-picking hologram—just sitting and muttering about wanting to see his lawyer and wondering why all the Boov were snickering at him.

"Why is everyone snickering at him?" I whispered to J.Lo.

"Ahyes," J.Lo said, twiddling his fingers. "'Lawyer' sounds just alike the Boovish word for these tiny face pumpkins we get."

"Tiny . . . what?"

"Every youngBoov, he is taught: 'If you're good and wash your face/Then you wills not gets the lawyers.'"

"Ah."

"It rhymes in Boovish."

"Neat."

"Emerson?" Landry was calling now. "Emerson? Come to Daddy."

But Emerson was standing apart, near J.Lo and me, trying to look like he didn't care. Which is impossible to pull off.

"Come *here*. Emerson? Emerson, you've got to get a message to Daddy's lawyers—hey! Stop that laughing!

I outrank you and I *order* you to stop laughing!"

And if the video footage weren't enough: soon Dark J.Lo woke up and started talking, and everyone realized that in *his* timeline it had been Smek and Landry's waveform device that caused all of New Boovworld to explode. Dark J.Lo seemed pretty psyched that it had never technically been his fault after all. And about equally embarrassed about all the assassination attempts.

"Ohhey, do not worry about it," J.Lo told him.

"I do, though," said Dark J.Lo. "I do worry about it."

"The important thing is that you did your best," J.Lo insisted.

The authorities were talking about putting Dark J.Lo in jail, but then regular J.Lo spoke up on his behalf, and in the end he got off with some community service. I hear he changed his name to Rihanna to avoid any confusion.

J.Lo and I sat together while they decided where to hold Smek. Rihanna had shot up one of their better prisons.

"How come it's so easy for us?" I asked J.Lo. "Staying friends, I mean. Sure, I got mad at you for a while, but we're good now, right?"

"Yes," said J.Lo, wiggling his legs.

"Well, *you* wanted to erase our whole timeline, and look at us. And yet I'm still a little mad at my mom for recording over a Gladys Knight cassette I had when I was six."

J.Lo looked pensive. "I am thinking," he said, "that we

are easy because you and me, we never did expect to understands each other. We are happily surprised every day to be friends at all. But with our own peoples . . . we cannot forgive their differentness."

"You can't hold me!" Landry was shouting. "I am an American citizen! And a best-selling author!"

A Boov in a white uniform approached J.Lo and me.

"Squealer," he said, and gave a little bow while snapping his fingers.

"J.Lo," said J.Lo.

"Of course. You will be taken to the HighBoov's private mansion to await next week's election. Anything you want will be yours."

"I want not to be taken to the HighBoov's private mansion to await next week's election," said J.Lo.

The Boov in white furrowed his face and looked back at the others. "This has never happened before," he said.

"I want to go home," said J.Lo.

"Ah!" said the Boov. "I did not realize. Do you have an apartment here in New Smek City, or—"

"My home is Earth," said J.Lo. "For now."

I exhaled. I hadn't been worried, but, you know. I'd been a *little* bit worried.

"Even though sometimes it's really hard there?" I asked.

"Home is where the hard is," said J.Lo. "As the humans say."

"No one says that." I smiled.

"There he is!" said someone, and we looked up to see a throng of Boov surging in from the reception room. "The Squealer!"

"He squeals for freedom!" shouted someone else. "And gun rights!"

"No he doesn't!" said a Boov wearing natural fibers. "He squeals for wildlife protection and recycling!"

The military police tried to hold them back, but a hundred Boov or more spilled into the room, some with signs.

"AAH!" squealed J.Lo, standing up on his chair as they came for him. "Heynow!"

They crowded around, pulled him down, then lifted him up over their heads.

"Stop that!" I shouted, reaching for J.Lo's arm. "Knock it off!" But they grabbed me, too.

"Humansgirl! Humansgirl! Look at my shirt slogan! It says 'Don't Be Afraid to Love'!"

"That's really flattering!" I shouted back. "Please put me down!"

And now they were separating us, parading J.Lo away, fighting over who got to carry him and what it meant if they did.

"Stop!" said J.Lo. "Please! Do not put your hand there!"

"J.Lo!" I said. "I don't know what to do!"

"Do not lets them take me!"

They passed him hand over hand. Toward the door
of the Oval Office they passed him, toward reception,
toward a tall figure standing in the entrance. A familiar
figure.

Everyone fell silent when they saw her, and froze.

"Mom?" I gasped.

"HEY!" Mom said, her face like something the Greeks
would have painted on a shield to frighten their enemies.
"TAKE. YOUR. *HANDS*. OFF. MY. *DAUGHTER*."

The Boov who had grabbed me quickly put me down and
stepped away.

"Sorry," one of them told me.

"Sorry."

"Sorry."

Mom thundered into the room, and now I could see
Ponch Sandhandler behind her.

"NOW WHERE IS J.LO?" asked Mom. J.Lo waggled his
hand. "I'M SORRY, J.LO, I COULDN'T TELL."

"Is okay."

"PUT HIM DOWN TOO."

"But," said a Boov, who probably wished he hadn't.

"BUT WHAT? BUT *WHAT*? MY NAME IS LUCY TUCCI
AND I HAVE DRIVEN EIGHT HUNDRED *MILLION* MILES
AND I DO *NOT* WANT TO HEAR ANY BACK TALK."

The Boov put J.Lo down.

"Sorry, Ms. Tucci," they mumbled, looking at their feet.

"Sorry, Ms. Tucci."

"Sorry."

I ran to her.

"I am *so* glad to see—"

"ZIP IT AND GET YOUR THINGS. WE ARE *LEAVING*."

I zipped it and grabbed J.Lo and Bill and rushed to her side. Emerson appeared there too.

"Ms. Tucci," he said, "can I get a ride?"

TWENTY-THREE

It was a long drive back.

Ponch Sandhandler arranged to get Slushious out of impound so we could fly her home to Earth. It was Sandhandler who had flown to Earth in the first place when J.Lo's initial broadcast had revealed that there was a human girl on New Boovworld. She-he had found my mom and brought her here. She-he was a good egg, Sandhandler.

So: Mom and J.Lo in the front seats, Emerson, Bill, and me in the back. For about the first hundred million miles I tried to get a conversation going with Mom, but she'd never liked airing our family business in front of strangers, and Emerson was in the car. So we all fell into this brittle silence, apart from J.Lo's nanowave radio.

". . . and after pulling the Boov to safety, that koobish was given a medal and had its ears eaten by a *very* famous chair designer. Back to you, Bish."

"Bish Bishley is taking some vacation time with a former coworker, Chad. This is Lala Hombalamilay filling in."

"Welcome aboard, Lala! Can you bring us the latest on the hunt for fugitive and former HighBoov Captain Smek?"

"The council is staying tight-lipped about both Captain Smek and the human Dan Landry, Chad, except to say that Landry is being held in Detention Nub Seven until they can consult with authorities on Earth. But secret sources tell us that after evading custody late last night, Captain Smek fled to his mansion atop the artificial hill known as Smek Peak— and would still be there now if the hill hadn't collapsed this morning from crumplepits."

"Interesting."

J.Lo turned down the volume. I was about to ask him to turn it up again when I heard Mom snoring in the front seat. So I stayed in the back, thinking.

I got to be there for the Chief when he passed. I'll always be glad about that. That morning he was looking better. I thought he was getting better. I didn't know he would die that afternoon.

He said, "I don't bet anyone gets to the end and says, 'I wish I'd kept my mouth shut.'" And then he paused to catch his breath and added, "No matter how much time you get, there's something you forgot to say."

From now on I'd leave nothing unsaid, I decided. From now on it was going to be easier at home thanks to all my incredible openness. So the rest of the way to Earth I practiced what I'd say to Mom, because I was dumb and thought practice would help.

For the last million miles the CHECK OIL light was on, but we still made it okay.

We dropped Emerson off at his mom's place, which meant taking a side trip to California.

"Your mom's gonna be surprised when you tell her all this," I said as he stepped out onto the curb.

Emerson turned. "Maybe not," he said. "She always says Dad'll end up in the White House or the Big House. I mean, she *always* says that. Like three times a day."

I smiled. "Friend me, okay?" I said. "And good luck."

Emerson glanced briefly at Mom, then me. "Good luck to *you*," he answered.

We waited until he was safely inside. Then forty minutes later we were descending over Pennsylvania, and home.

We landed in the driveway. Before the dust settled Mom was already in the yard, stomping toward the house, one shoe in hand and eyes like a cartoon owl. She got the front door open and Lincoln bounded out of it, knocking her over—like a *Marmaduke* comic strip, but funny. And now Lincoln was barking, running around and around the car and then jumping inside when we opened the doors. Pig came out onto the front step, looked at us like she'd just now realized we'd been gone, and went back inside.

I came up to Mom, smirking at how she'd landed butt-first in the flower bed, but then she shot me a look and I put that smirk *away*. This was *not* the part of the story where we both laughed despite ourselves and realized that Everything Was Going to Be Okay.

Then, suddenly, Mom rocked forward and hugged me. She hugged me in a way that was kind of terrifying, actually, and pushed me out to look at me. And hugged me again.

"I know," I said. "I'm grounded."

"Oh, you do *not* know," she hissed. I realize there aren't any *s* sounds in there, but I swear she hissed all the same. "You've never even *heard* of grounding like this. A person could *die* from this much grounding."

"I just . . . Life is short and I want you to know that I love you and I always will, and . . . things are going to be better now, I promise—"

"Oh, for God's sake, Gratuity, you don't get to talk your way out of this! (Pardon my language.) You screwed up *way* too big this time!"

Mom was barking, so I guess Lincoln thought it was a good time to start barking too. He licked us and put his paws on us and barked until Mom stuck out her arm.

"Lincoln! In the house!"

Lincoln went in the house. Bill flew around and around, writing a whole novel over our front yard. I think we were making him nervous.

I quailed a little. "I'm . . . not trying to talk my way out of it. I'm trying to talk *through*—"

"Nope! I give you all this credit for being *so mature*, so *wise* for your age, but you're the same thirteen-year-old sneaking out with her boyfriend that I was!"

I put my hands up. "Okay, *waitaminute*. Credit? *You* give me credit? Do you not remember what I've done? I earned my *own* credit. I should have a *giant credit card* made out of regular-sized credit cards, I have so much credit."

Mom pursed her lips. "This from the girl who says she *doesn't want anyone to know*—"

"Oh man . . ." I said, and I broke down a little. "Oh man, of *course* I want people to know! Are you kidding me? I want every single person to know!"

I flailed my arms and fell backward onto the grass.

"*I saved the world*. I should get to turn in homework late because *I saved the world.* That girl Stephanie shouldn't make fun of my hair clips anymore, because *I saved the world.*"

I felt dizzy. It felt good to admit this, despite the circumstances.

"I . . . want everyone to treat me like a regular person," I finished. "A regular person that they think is *amazing.*"

Mom actually looked like she felt sorry for me for a moment. That seemed like a good sign. She sat down in the grass too.

"So I guess deep down I expect all this credit for taking care of myself all those years," I said, and Mom looked down. "But instead you're all SuperMom lately, and I like it and hate it at the same time."

"That's normal," said Mom. "That's how you're supposed to feel about being parented."

"I guess. I guess I just . . . I decided recently that I maybe have trouble trusting . . . things, and—"

"And so you've been testing me," said Mom. "Oh, believe me, Gratuity, I know."

I flinched—*I* hadn't even known. But as soon as she said it, I realized it was true.

"Well, but I'm done doing that!" I said quickly. "Things are going to be better now!"

Mom sighed.

"Things are not going to just 'be better' now, Gratuity," she said. "Things are gonna pretty much be lousy for a while. And I am so, so proud of what you did in the invasion, but I still get to treat you like a little girl, because you are a little girl and that's my *right*."

I didn't like that. But I remembered my talks with the Chief and decided not to do the idiot thing.

"It's going to get worse," Mom said, "'cause that's how

it is. And you're gonna hate me a little in your teens. Like, legitimately hate me."

"Wha . . . no," I said. "You know I love you—"

"Oh, and you think you can't do both at the same time? Love and hate? You can totally do both, Gratuity! Get ready! And when you go off to college, you'll say mean things about me to your new friends—unfair things, because you'll *all* hate your parents. You and your friends will have *invented* hating your parents. And . . . you'll learn so much and go so many places, places I never could go. So you'll think you're better than me." She took my face in her hands, smiling suddenly. "And you'll be better than me—you'll be so much better than me."

Her eyes were wet; her cheeks were stained. I knew my face looked like her face.

"Later, you'll call more," she said. "And visit. You'll be, like . . . *amazed* when you realize I'm right about a few things. I'll be like a horse who can do math. Maybe later still you'll have a daughter and realize how . . . just . . . screwed up and hopeless we all are."

She let go of me and leaned back.

"And eventually you and me'll get to be friends again, kind of. Like school friends who were always seated together because we have the same last name. You never would have chosen me, but now . . . why not, you know?"

We were quiet. I heard only the birds, and the *tick-tick-tick* of the car engine cooling.

"Well. That . . . sounds *awful*," I said, and we both laughed.

"Yeah," Mom agreed. "Pretty awful."

She smiled.

"You wanna do it anyway?" She extended a hand.

I took it.

And she was wrong, you know. I didn't tell her then, so I would have to remember to tell her again and again, for the rest of our lives: I would've chosen her. I was choosing her now.

Anyway.

After a longish hug, J.Lo cleared his throat and waved from the driveway.

"I also am here," he said.

* * *

I'm making all this sound easier than it was. She was mad for a long time.

But we survived.

But I'm *still* grounded.

We hear Funsize is doing well—after a long vacation with an old friend, he was put in charge of overhauling the whole New Boovworld sanitation system. It's a big job, but he's going to have a lot of help. In particular, he has a Boov and a human who've been sentenced to work as garbagemen, so they pretty much have to do whatever he says. They both used to be in politics.

But that's not even the biggest news.

A few days after we got home, the election was held on New Boovworld. J.Lo won.

The Boov decided that the second-place winner should act as president if the fairly elected president of New Boovworld is away. And by an almost unanimous write-in vote, the second-place winner ended up being Ponch Sandhandler.

And the fairly elected president of New Boovworld *is* away, is eight hundred million *miles* away, and currently in my kitchen spreading rubber cement on a doughnut.

"Hey, Mr. President!" I called.

J.Lo leaned into the door frame. "Ohyes, hello?"

Lincoln lay at my feet. Pig chased Bill across the living room.

"You wanna go down to the lake and throw rocks, Mr. President?" I asked.

J.Lo nodded solemnly, or tried to.

"I . . . command that it be so," he declared, then burst out laughing.

APPENDIX A: Rules for Stickyfish

Stickyfish (from the Old Boovish, *ztikifitch*) is, in modern times, the most widely played Boovish sport. It is based on a four-thousand-year-old historical conflict between the two great nations of Boovworld (before all Boov were united under the HighBoov). The conflict arose over which nation was the rightful owner of the mythical stickyfish. Each wanted the other to have it. It smelled.

You'll need a supply of fish. Balloonafish will do. If no balloonafish, water balloons or a plain ball or Koosh may be substituted.

Players form two teams, or nations.

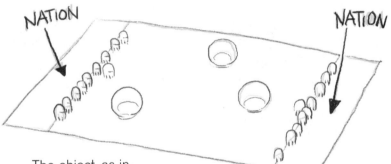

The object, as in American football, is to move the "stickyfish" into your opponent's end zone (or nation). Moving the stickyfish into your opponent's nation scores one "haboobi."

The team with the most haboobis after a set time has elapsed wins the match. Under the variant Bigfield Rules there is no time limit, and the first team to score a predetermined number of haboobis wins the match.

Team captains play fat-flat-bitey to determine first possession of the stickyfish (fat beats bitey; bitey beats flat; flat beats fat). Each team then lines up on its own national border. Play begins with a signal from the referee.

The fish carrier and her team advance down the field. The fish may be thrown any number of times to other members of the offense.

Members of the defense may NOT touch the stickyfish, even when it is being thrown. There are no "pass interceptions." They may not touch any member of the offense who is not, at that moment, carrying the stickyfish. Unless that person is singing (see below).

They may distract an offensive member and cause her to fail to catch a pass, however, as long as they touch neither the player nor the fish.

If the fish carrier is two-hand touched by a member of the defense, or if the stickyfish is allowed by the offense to touch the ground, then play ends and the fish is left on that spot.

The defense now takes possession and becomes the offense, and the opposing team lines up on its national border. Play resumes at the referee's signal.

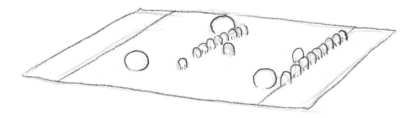

If the teams are playing with an actual fish or with a water balloon, and the fish or balloon bursts, play is halted while a replacement is prepared. Then the defense takes possession at the spot on which the fish/balloon burst, as above.

The referee will place three large bubbles on the field as shown in the previous diagrams. If bubbles are not available, these spots may be marked however you wish, but they should be no larger than three feet square. These places are safetybubbles, and a fish carrier who enters a safetybubble cannot be touched by the defense until she leaves it. The fish carrier may throw to other members of the offense from the safety of the safetybubble.

The fish carrier may stay within the safetybubble indefinitely. However—if she is still inside and a member of the defense enters a DIFFERENT safetybubble and shouts "Safetybubbletrouble!" then play ends and possession switches, as above.

At any point during play a member of the offense who does not have possession of the stickyfish may run into the opposing team's end zone and sing the following song:

Stickyfish, O stickyfish,
You pink 'n stinkin' icky fish,
O please accept my invitation
to this really awesome nation.

The singer must remain in the end zone for the full duration of the song.

Members of the defense may attempt to two-hand touch the singer—if they do so before the end of the song, then the stickyfish declines the invitation and play continues normally. If the singer makes a mistake (as judged by the referee) while singing, the stickyfish declines the invitation and play continues normally. In either case, no member of that team may sing again until that team's next possession.

Regardless, play continues normally while the song is being sung, so if the player in possession of the stickyfish is two-hand touched before the end of the song, play ends and the defense takes possession.

But! If the offensive player successfully sings the entire song before she or the fish carrier is two-hand touched, then play ends and the stickyfish accepts the invitation, thereby scoring one haboobi for the offense. The defense becomes the offense and takes possession on its own national border.

APPENDIX B: J.LO in: "Smektastic Voyage"

MAIL!

Is there something for me? Is there?

Weird—there is.

Number-one champion!

What is it?

You've been asked to be a presenter at the Latin Grammys.

Sorry, J.Lo, it's just another mistake.

J.Lo was impatient to go public. He wanted to announce his alien Boov self to the whole world, not just to our family and close neighbors who knew about him already. He was getting good at reading and writing and had two e-mail addresses and his own page on MySpace, which he'd originally thought was about astronomy.

Every once in a while I'd catch him in some chat room typing

I am a three-foots-tall alien named J.Lo

but someone would type back

I am a 12th level half-elven ranger named Ganthemede

so it hadn't been a real problem yet.

Then, somehow, between all the chat rooms and blog comments and his habit of filling out every Customer Feedback form and Sweepstakes Entry he could get his mittens on...

...he'd landed on some mailing list as the other J.Lo, the human J.Lo, and since then a few letters had arrived. On our front table was a stack of fan mail and an invitation to the wedding of the Vice President of Paramount.

Maybies...I could go see these Latin Grannies. Maybies without my ghost costume.

Ummmmmm, no. It's going to be televised. The world isn't ready.

Look at this cover story. This guy is saying the Boov should give us all this stuff. He want resp... ...what was it? ...reparations. He wants them to announce that they committed "crimes against humanity and Boovanity" and broadcast it to the whole galaxy.

CARNIVAL SUNDAY

MAKING THEM PAY

And this is the same magazine that holds an America's Cutest Puppy contest three times a year.

I love that contest.

Great. Anyway. You see my point?

ADAM REX

is the *New York Times* best-selling author and illustrator of *Frankenstein Makes a Sandwich*. His other books include *Pssst!*, *Moonday*, *The True Meaning of Smekday*, *Fat Vampire*, and *Cold Cereal*. He also illustrated the Brixton Brothers series, *Billy Twitters and His Blue Whale Problem*, and *Chloe and the Lion*, all by Mac Barnett, and *Chu's Day* by Neil Gaiman. He lives in Tucson, Arizona. Visit him at adamrex.com or follow him on Twitter @MrAdamRex.